DREAMS

COME TRUE II

IN THE STRUGGLE FINDING HOPE

BY

APRIL P WILLIAMS

Dreams Come True II: In the struggle finding hope

Published by PRELLA BOOKS

JERSEY CITY, NEW JERSEY

WILLIAMS, APRIL, Author DREAMS COME TRUE II APRIL WILLIAMS

ISBN: 978-0-578-29934-1

QUANTITY PURCHASES: Schools, companies, professional groups, clubs, and other organizations may qualify for special terms when ordering quantities of this title.

For information, email April.Smiles@Hotmail.com.

Love letter and Dedication

This letter is to the soldiers, veterans and people who are in the struggle looking for hope. There is an old adage that says: *"the squeaky wheel gets the grease, but no one ever talks about the quiet wheel that falls off. No one pays attention to know if the quiet wheel is in trouble too.*

There are times when life gets in the way and you feel like you have no choice but to take it. Then here comes the negative thoughts that creeps up into your mind saying, "You are not good enough." "Maybe they are right;" "You are a failure." "You should be ashamed of yourself." "You're too old." Whatever it is! You are the one that tells everyone that everything is going to be okay not knowing you are a quiet wheel! You are in danger. Not just from life getting in the way but, from yourself because you are now starting to believe there is no hope.

In that split second when you think that all hope is gone, you, "the quiet wheel," starts to fall off. Save yourself by removing yourself from people, places, and things that hurt your mental health. Remember these scriptures: "*For our struggle is not against flesh and blood, but against the rulers, against the authorities, against the powers of this dark world and against the spiritual forces of evil in the heavenly realms.* (Ephesians 6:12) *We walk by faith and not by sight.* 2 Corinthians 5:7 *I can do all things through Christ who strengthens me.* Philippians 4:13

Continue to talk to God to get yourself through the negative thoughts. At those critical moments, find someone to talk to, even if it's a stranger. Just talk to someone, who can get you to see things from a different point of view that'll keep you, "the wheel," from falling off and help you to find hope again.

With utmost love in my heart, I want to thank you, all Soldiers and Veterans for your service and my mom for sharing her story. Mona Starr Goodrum Dunn.

(July 13, 1942 - November 1, 2022) I love you mommy.

Warm and loving hugs,

April P Williams

Friend, let me help you...As you will find this story fascinating: Intrigued, by listening to, "A Stroke of Insight, by Dr. Jill Bolte Taylor" She sucked me in and I was captivated by her detailed oriented experience of having a stroke. A brain injury. She revisited painful but, yet mesmerizing memories of that dreadful day second by second to give us a full view of her encounter. She highlighted that during her recovery she had no memory. She could not remember anything. Then I instantly thought of when the Bible speaks of being transformed by the renewing of your mind. She had no more anger, shame, disappointment, hate, years of stress. It had all gone away. Why? She just didn't remember. Her mind had been renewed. A clean slate. She gets to form new beliefs and spread love and positive energy. Imagine how a renewed mind can help begin to heal your body. That is why you have to heal the mind with healing the body, I came to believe. It's tricky. How do you get your serenity back or how do you deal with gut wrenching memories? It takes time, work and help to get there. There is hope.

You are not alone...

Reach out to: NA: 866-977-9213/ AA: 800-839-1686

Gamblers Anonymous
Text or call: 800-522-4700
Suicide hotline-800-273-8255
BetterHelp.com

Why I was inspired to write this story

It was February 26, 1993. A bomb blast went off in the garage of the World Trade Center, and my mother, Mona Dunn was in the WTC. She worked (Fiduciary Trust) on the 94th floor in one of the towers. As that bomb went off, killing and injuring people. The survivors had to scamper out for safety. Some children had come to visit the building on that fateful day. They too, just like my mom, were in the building when it happened.

My mom watched these children as she walked down 94 flights of stairs. The children were encouraged by their teachers to keep going even though they were tired and had to go to the bathroom. These children inspired my mom to keep going down the stairs with them. She said that at that moment, even when she felt exhausted, she said to herself that *"if these children can walk down all of these stairs, I can too."*

Then came that horrific morning of September 11, 2001. Yes, my mother was also there. She was a part of the "Fiduciary Trust Company," Her work family. She was on the 96th floor when the first plane hit. My mom made her way down to the 78th floor. While on the 78th floor, she said that her boss, Eleonora Halton suggested that they should both go down and get out of the building.

Right then, my mom remembered that she forgot her pocketbook on the 94th floor. She said she needed to go back up to get it. Eleonora or Nora everyone called her suggested for her to leave the pocketbook for now and go back later to get it. Mom agreed.

The elevator door opened at that moment; they got in and headed down. And as they got off the elevator and went through the revolving doors in the lobby, they heard the second plane hit the building!

My mom, still inside the WTC, cringed when she heard the crash but she didn't know what was going on until they got outside. Fearing not to get hit by falling debris she was told by the police when to run to get across the street. Finally across the street she saw scores of people running, screaming, crying and panicked as they scampered for safety. As she looked up in her mind's eye she saw people falling out of the building but their spirits were caught by angels. Her eyes and mouth opened wide in shock, as she imagined what could have happened if Nora didn't insist that they get out of the building at that very moment they did. Because of this, even till this day, my mom still calls Nora her "Angel."

The sounds of cries of agony, the wailing sound of people gritting in pain, and the roaring of a raging fire consuming the building, all towered the blaring sirens from police cars, fire trucks and ambulances. My mom could not bear to see anymore so she turned around and started walking with a heart-wrenching bitter taste of dust in her throat. She was confused and terrified. Who would have ever thought the buildings would come down.

Sometime later on, news broke that the military had set out to an unknown land and culture to put boots on the ground to find and destroy the people who were behind these devastating acts. That day, I felt a connection with each individual soldier that had enormous courage to fight for us Americans who were left broken and devastated. I felt like these *soldiers said to Americans "don't panic. We got you."*

How do I express my gratitude and show my appreciation to all of you soldiers? Many soldiers who came back were devastated and distraught emotionally. Many soldiers who came back disabled paralyzed, crushed physically and many soldiers who gave the ultimate, their life. Leaving their spouses, children, parents, siblings and friends behind. As a daughter that had a parent in that building I was flooded with an anonymous amount of fears from that dreadful day. How do I liberate myself from this anguish that secretly keeps appearing in my life?

I stumbled upon a remedy to release the boiling water on the inside of me that I felt was building into trapped steam. I started writing! I could feel the pressure being released and oozing out of me with each stroke of the key to my laptop. Finally, I can say "Thank you" and give this gift of a story to the soldiers and veterans who read this story about a soldier now a veteran who just came back from Afghanistan and is trying to find his way back into civilian life. Just when he thought he finished the fight. Here comes another one. This story is a gift of finding hope to anyone who really needs hope right now. I felt guided by the Holy Spirit while writing this story. I'm sending each one of you soldiers and veterans a warm and loving hug. Thank you for your service...

The author who brought you,

Dreams Come True: Winning is possible with the first move.

Presents

Dreams Come True II: In the Struggle Finding Hope.

Dreams Come True II

In the struggle finding for hope

Prella Books

TABLE OF CONTENTS

Afghanistan

"How did I get here?" I wondered as I reflected through the last four years I've been in the army. I needed to get out of there. When I was enlisting for the military, I did not envisage that I would be deployed to Afghanistan for twenty months out of my first four years. The stress was relentless. It was a total culture shock. No running water, no electricity, no sewage. The heat was almost unbearable. The nights were unforgivingly cold and when the wind blew, it carried with it all kinds of sharp sand that bit my skin.

I never realized how much I depended on cell phones and computers until I got to Afghanistan where there were none. We were surrounded by mountains and sand, and we got into many fights with the Taliban. I started to feel like I was playing Russian roulette with my life.

I remember one night when I was out on patrol inside of the US combat outpost. I was talking to Sergeant Ronald Smith, a black man who knew who he was and who's he was, a devout Christian. He was a few years older than me, and I dare say he was wiser too. He came from the streets of Newark, NJ and wanted a better life so he joined the Army over eight years ago. He was stationed in North Carolina with his wife Nicole, a kindergarten schoolteacher and his six-year-old daughter Tracy whose pictures he carries with him all the time. He was looking forward to having a son one day.

I will never forget our last conversation. It was a clear and brisk night. The stars were bright in the sky, and we were sitting down talking and trying to stay warm.

"Hey sarge, did I ever tell you why I joined the army?"

"No, he replied."

"Well, I'll tell you," I said, jokingly. "It was about a year after September 11th. When the World Trade Center was attacked. I had done one year at Virginia State University. While I was there, my roommate from New York lost his mother in one of the towers. He was devastated and needed someone to talk to. I was there for him, so we became friends, and we talked about his mom all the time. He didn't know his dad. His mom was the one paying his way through school, so as she had died, he wasn't sure he would be able to come back the next year.

He felt so all alone. I could hear him crying at night. Each night I felt so bad for him. When we returned for our sophomore year, he didn't come back. I became so angry that my friend just had his future snatched from his hands, so without thinking about it I decided to join the army. I wanted to find this guy named Osama bin Laden who was responsible for devastating the lives of so many people."

He looked at me with disbelief.

"I didn't even know this guy," I continued. "He came from a country that I didn't even know anything about." I paused and took a deep breath as all those emotions came flooding back to me. "Why do you think Osama bin Laden and Al-Qaeda did this to us, Sarge?" I asked, looking at his face like an inquisitive child asking his father questions.

"Well, Mack," Sarge began. We would have to go back to the 1930s. Before you and I were born. There was an oil company in the United States that was looking to find more oil. They had a hunch that maybe, just maybe, they'd be able to find oil in Saudi Arabia. Saudi Arabia is a Muslim country and their land it's very sacred to them. They don't care for non-Muslim Americans that don't share their beliefs and respect their lifestyle. Our lifestyle is very different from theirs. Their land is Holy and they believe only Muslims can be there. So, this oil company went to the Saudi Arabian royal family and told them that they think there is oil there in Saudi Arabia. The Americans asked them if they could explore their sacred land by drilling to see if they could find some oil. They told them that they could both become extremely rich if they eventually find oil in their country. Hmmm, the Royal family thought about it and said, "Okay." So, the Saudi's Royal family, who really didn't want non-muslims Americans in their country, agreed. So, after a few years, Americans found oil in a place called Dhahran in Saudi Arabia."

As I was listening to Sarge, I was becoming impatient to know how all of this relates to my question, so I asked him, "Ok? but what does that have to do with September 11, 2001?"

"Well to make the long story short," Sarge continued, "The United States wanted to build a military base to protect the oil and the Americans that lived and worked there. The Saudi's royal family wasn't crazy about the idea but they were getting rich. So they agreed again. But they needed someone to build it. So, the Saudis and the Americas agreed to hire a man by the name of Mohammed who had a contracting business that built infrastructure and real estate. This man became extremely rich because of all of the work . This guy Mohammed had a lot of wives and children. We don't get down like that in the United States but, that's their custom. Anyway, he had around fifty-four kids."

"Wait! I'm sorry I have to stop you right there," I said in shock. "Fifty-four kids?"

"Yep," he answered, smiling as I shook my head in disbelief. "Well, each of his children became very rich also."

"Wow," I bellowed out, trying to imagine what fifty-four stinkingly rich siblings would look like.

"So, one of Mohammed bin Laden's sons is named Osama bin Laden."

"What?" I exclaimed, and at that moment, I realized that I hadn't paid attention to the contractor's name- Mohammed bin Laden.

"Yeah," Sarge nodded. "I'm not sure how the story goes but he hated the Americans that came to live in their Holy land drilling for oil. They were staying too long. Osama was a strict Muslim whose goal was to protect Islam from big world powers by violently striking back at countries that infiltrated their land. So, Osama went to the Royal family in Saudi Arabia and told them that he really doesn't want the Americans there. But the Royal family and others involved in the business were making a crazy amount of money. Like billionaire money. So, they told Osama to relax and let them stay. Anyway, Russia was a keen observer watching how Saudi Arabia and the United States were getting rich. So, they started inching their way over to Afghanistan, to take over, I guess. So, Osama bin Laden left Saudi Arabia and went to Afghanistan, and there he formed a group called Al-Qaeda. The United States gave Osama and Al-Qaeda money to help fund the war between Russia and Afghanistan."

"Wait," I interrupted again, "Are you saying that America gave Osama bin Laden money?"

"Well, yes. I believe," he replied. "The United States was indirectly protecting the oil they had found in Saudi Arabia."

"Okay, so what happened? My curiosity peaked.

Sarge smiled hearing the eagerness in my voice. "After 10 years or so, Russia retreated. As you can see, there are a lot of mountains and caves here in Afghanistan. As it seemed like normalcy was about to be restored, there came Saddam Hussain, the dictator of Iraq. He was trying to take over Kuwait, and while at it, he was getting a little too close to Saudi Arabia, and too close to the oil. The same oil that America and Saudi were benefiting from; the same oil that has somehow made even Saddam Hussain a lot of money. So, Osama bin Laden came back to where he was born in Saudi Arabia. He wanted to fight Saddam Hussein. He felt he was a ruthless dictator who was going to take over Kuwait. But the Royal family said, *"No, we will get the Americans to fight them for us. They have more resources than you and al-Qaeda."* But Osama bin Laden said, *"we fought Russia and won!"* The Royal family argued that it was because of the terrain. They reminded him that there are no mountains and caves in Kuwait, unlike Afghanistan. Now, Osama bin Laden became really pissed that the royal family trusted the Americans to do a better job at protecting Kuwait and fighting Saddam Hussein more than him and Al-Qaeda. So he started attacking Americans all over the world— I guess to prove a point of how powerful he and al-Qaeda was. I think the World Trade Center represented to him the financial district of the United States and where can you cripple the economy, provoke the most fear, cause death? In buildings that have thousands of people in it. Osama and

Al-Qaeda have made their presence known to the United States on our soil and there's hell to pay for that.

"Wow, Sarge I never knew that but I'm still confused. We made Saudi Arabia and his father rich. Which made Osama bin Laden rich, so the United States was not his enemy. So, please don't tell me it was about Osama bin Laden's ego not being stroked by Saudi Arabia that made him attack the United States" I said. I was beginning to feel too cold, so I got up to find somewhere else to sit down to get warm. "Let me ask you a question, Sarge."

"Yeah," he said as he followed me to find a place to sit and keep warm.

"Do you think we will ever find Osama bin Laden?" I asked, waiting for his words of wisdom that never came because at that very moment, I heard a machine gun, followed by a painful thud on the ground. I turned and saw him on the ground, the very place I stood as I saw his blood gushing out. I froze. I couldn't move a muscle. I heard a loud voice saying, "Incoming! Incoming! Incoming! Border attack! Border attack!"

I could hear mortar explosives coming at us at lightning speed.

"Oh Shit! They are getting closer," someone shouted out.

I could hear machine guns going off nonstop *Brrrrrrrrrrrrrrr*! Tat, tat, tat! and I just stood there trying to figure out what just happened.

"Incoming! Incoming! Incoming!" Soldiers screamed out at every corner! And then I felt this force; this sudden burst of energy, violently moving from one side of my being to the other. My spirit was shaken in fear, and it felt like it was looking for a way to burst out of my body. It was only my skin that kept my spirit trapped inside my body.

As I stood there transfixed in the middle of the rapid fire, Within seconds I felt another soldier grab me from behind and yanked me to a corner. Immediately, I saw machine gun bullets splutter around that spot where I was. "Oh, my God" I stammered. My entire body was quivering in fear, and at that instant, I forgot that I had a M4 Carbine. At that moment, I just wanted to go home where I could be safe. But that was not an option.

When things got a little quiet, I could hear someone say in a low tone, "anyone hit? Anyone hit?"

"Over here, I shouted as low as I could, pointing at Sarge, with tears trailing down my eyes. Then suddenly, fear turned into a fight! I was angry they had just killed Sarge and other guys I considered my brothers! Brrrrrrrrrrrrrrr. The shooting started up again. I grabbed my weapon and launched into full-blown assault. *Brrrrrrrrrrrrrrrrrrr!* Tat,tat,tat! My fingers clenched hard against the trigger, purring bullets at the enemies. Soon I could hear the hovering sound of CH- 47F chinook helicopters coming from a distance. On seeing that our backup had arrived, the Taliban started to flee. At that very moment, I knew that I had just become a man. One year later, it was time for me to reenlist back into the army, I just couldn't do it anymore. Joining the Army was never my plan in life anyway.

Suicidal Without Warning

On getting back to North Carolina, I couldn't find a salary paying job with benefits anywhere. Today, it felt as if I'm wearing the cloak of bad luck all over me. Everywhere I turned, all I got was rejection after rejection. *"I'm sorry Mr. Mack, you don't have any experience for this job. Come back when you have more experience."*

"Oh, I'm sorry Mr. Mack, we are looking for someone with a college degree."

"Yes, Mr. Mack, we just filled that position earlier today."

"Oh, Mr. Mack, you have too much experience."

"I'm sorry Mr. Mack I don't think this position is a good fit for you."

Then finally the last job interview of the day. I'm looking in the eyes of this arrogant white privileged man, and he is looking back at me condescendingly with a smirk. "I'm sorry we have more qualified applicants than you," he said, glancing at my application. "What's your name again? He asked. "Oh yeah, Danny Mack. You can see your way out."

I just looked at this man and shook my head as I thought to myself *"I have stared fear right back in the eyes. I have seen death all around me," "I have risked my life so that you can sit behind that bougie desk and have the luxury of blowing me off."*

American civilians take for granted the privilege of being able to go to work in an office building without worrying if their office complex would be the next building to be blown up by al-Qaeda, Isis, the Taliban or whoever, and they will never understand what soldiers and their families have to live with every day. These families are constantly quietly living in fear that their loved ones may never come home alive. We put our lives on the line for this country so it can be the "United States of America."

I left the building in a hurry, feeling deflated, embarrassed and humiliated. I couldn't help but mumble in frustration saying, "Oh Lord, I reacted off of my emotions and made the wrong choice by joining the military. Have I made a mistake that I can't recover from?"

Leaving the last interview of the day. I felt humiliated, lost, and ashamed of myself in front of the people who interviewed me. But I have been trained not to let it show. As I get into my car. I just sit here, thinking of where I could find the nearest cliff to drive off of. I turned on the engine, swerved into reverse and pulled off recklessly, nearly hitting a parked car. I could hardly see due to the tears streaming down my face. I can't trust my own feelings. I feel like I betrayed myself. All I could hear was the yelling and screaming in my head. At first, I thought it was someone else yelling at me, but when I realized that it was me yelling and screaming out loud, my body began to quiver.

With my foot pressed hard against the accelerator, I did not know how fast I was driving, but I knew that I didn't mind if the car started to fly. I looked up and saw the yellow light up ahead, but I didn't care. I'm driving too fast to stop. I want to end it all. Then out of nowhere, I saw a woman and a child walking across the street. I saw just a few feet away from sweeping them both off the ground. Without thinking, my foot moved to the brake and pressed hard on it. The car jerked and with a loud stretching noise, it froze a few inches away from the woman and her child. I could see the horror on their faces.

"What the fuck is wrong with you?? Are you fucking crazy? You almost hit us!" The woman's voice rang out with fear and anger. "Stop driving so damn fast!" she spit as she hurried to the sidewalk with her child.

"I'm sorry! I'm sorry!" I shouted back at them with a trembling voice. I slammed my hand against the steering wheel crying out "I hate my life!" Suddenly, I heard loud honking sounds behind me. "The light is green!" Bellowed out a frustrated, irritable driver.

"Okay, okay!" I yelled back. "I'm moving!" I moved a bit and pulled over to the curb. I just sat there breathing fast and trying to calm down and get clarity.

"I just lost my fuckin mind! I almost killed two people. Oh Shit! I gotta get a grip on myself," I cried. I felt like I was still at war but this battle was letting these people get into my head. I was letting fear and hopelessness take over in my mind. After a few minutes, I started to think about the few good things that were happening for me, and then I pulled off ever so slowly calming down to make my way to the Community Center where my nephews Lucas and Liam go to hang out after school.

They do their homework there, after which they learn how to play chess.

They didn't come there today, but it will be my first day volunteering. Thank God for coach Matthew. He coaches the basketball team at the Community Center.

Each time he saw me waiting for my nephews to finish playing chess, he would walk up to me to say hello. Then one day we just started talking and he invited me to help out with the boys on the team. He suggested that I tell the team a story or two about me being in the military. I think he was just trying to give me something to do while I waited for my nephews. I was so grateful he asked. I finally felt like I was needed for something.

I have been out of the military for almost a year now. I didn't realize how desperately I needed to feel needed.

So, I gladly accepted his offer. It gave me some of my dignity back.

"Good morning, Coach Matthew. I'm here," I greeted him with a smile as I got to the community center. "This is my first day and I am here to help you out any way I can. I just want to thank you for trusting me to talk to your boys."

"You are a veteran Danny," he said. "You have a lot of stories and wisdom to share. These kids need you."

"Thank you, Coach." I nodded.

"Well, they are out there. I will introduce you to them. Then I will let you take the floor. I'll be out later to get practice started," he said as he made me follow him out into this big orange and blue gymnasium. I could see the boys throwing hoops.

"Boys I want you to come over here," yelled Coach Matthew, "I have someone here who I want you to meet," the kids ran up to us and surrounded us. "His name is Mr. Mack. He was in the Army and now he is here to give you some wisdom and share some of his stories. Okay, Mr. Mack you got the floor. And then he leaned in and whispered, "Don't be nervous, you got this."

I smiled nervously. I had no clue of what I was going to say. "Thank you, Coach Matthew." I swallowed hard and smiled at the boys as they all sat down around me. "Boys, I really don't know what to say. It wasn't long ago that I was your age. So much has happened to me from when I was your age to this moment. I thought I had it all together. I wanted to be rich. Anybody here want to be rich?" I asked.

"Yes! Yes!" they all echoed, smiling.

"Yeah, me too. But, I had some lessons to learn first. I joined the Army right after one year of college, so I could find Osama bin Laden who had an army called Al-Qaeda. He and his army were the ones that were responsible for the attack on the World Trade Center. My plan was to come back and finish college but I've had a hard time trying to concentrate. I didn't realize that when I came back, I would be different from the way I was when I left. Life experiences have a way of changing your perspective about life. While I was in the army, I was trained to take orders, then climb the ranks. Life is mapped out for you. Just follow the system that's been set up for your success. Being a part of the military was exciting and rewarding. You are taught about brotherhood and being a team player. It's about being there for one another to win. Getting back home from war the same way I went to war, became riches for me."

I gave a half-smile as I realized that the kids don't seem to get my point. The truth is that I felt mentally and spiritually crushed. I could feel myself drifting away in thought for a second, so I caught myself and shifted my focus back to the kids.

"Now I have come to learn that having my life mapped out by the military system is not the direction I wanted to go. Coming back out into the civilian world you have to find your own path. There are no guarantees you will be hired for a job. The civilian system is ruthless. No one teaches brotherhood. No one teaches you to depend on one another and work as a team, so that we will all win.

There is no straight path to riches without its ups and downs. Now you're in a game where you have to figure out what the rules are and how to play and win. What does winning look like to you?" I asked, pointing at the boys.

"We told you Mr. Mack. We want to be rich!" some of them said.

"Yes, you did," I said, "but you need to know that the path won't be clear." There are a lot of paths out here in life. Some will lead you to win and some will lead you to lose. Now life becomes tricky when you are faced with choices. Making the wrong choice could lead you to lose. So, my goal is to give you food for thought and words of wisdom that I have learned along the way, to hopefully help you make better choices so you can win. Some things you will understand now and maybe there will be some things you will realize later. But today. I want you to understand this. You can become rich in many different ways. You may need to get a skill in addition to basketball. There are rich black people who started a roofing business. There are those who got rich from going into gardening for big companies and developments in the city. There are rich black people who own Porter potty businesses. They rent them out to businesses that are working in public places. If you learn how to code or hire someone who can code, you can develop an app. You can get rich owning real estate. There are so many ways to become rich. So don't get discouraged or lose hope. And fellas, being part of a team you have to be there for one another in order to win. No matter what team you belong to. Thank you guys for listening to a young, old man," I said as I concluded my talk. "Coach Matthew will be out soon."

"Thanks, Mr. Mack," the boys yelled out as they went back to throwing the basketball.

Lola's House

As I pulled into the driveway in front of the house, I saw my nephews playing chess on the big wrap around porch. The porch had two swings benches facing each other, hanging from the ceiling of the porch and surrounded by decorative potted red, yellow and white Poinsettias. It looked like a farmhouse. My older sister Lola loved this house so much, so I helped her buy it with my VA loan. It was a gift I got for her during my second year in the army. Two years after that, she became a Registered Nurse. Now she works as a registered nurse at the same medical clinic nearby where she used to work before.

She has been making all of the mortgage payments from day one. She finally got married a year later to her boyfriend, a general contractor named Evan. They have been together for thirteen years in total now with two beautiful sons. Evan makes a lot of money from his business, so he took over the mortgage payments and the house will be paid off in about ten years. Now, he is working on a new school building across town.

Evan is so loving and loyal to my sister. I love the way he loves my sister, and he is really understanding, and he doesn't mind that I have been stuck with them for the past ten months. Since I came out of the army it has been hard for me to stay focused. Sometimes, I kept drifting back to Afghanistan. It drove me crazy, and I wished I could control it.

Getting out of the car and walking towards the stairs to the porch, I just smiled at the sight of the boys, and then I thought, "*wow, just yesterday they were babies. Now Lucas is 12 years old and Liam is 11 years old.*"

"Hey, Uncle Danny," Lucas said, flashing a handsome smile.

He is just like his father. Lucas loves helping out and fixing things around the house. Seeing how dedicated he is to being crafty, his father signed him up for a shop class to keep him busy. There, he learned how to build model houses, and with time, it could become his new obsession.

Liam, on the other hand, loves to draw houses while Lucas tries to build them. Evan brought Lucas and Liam a 3D build house kit and has been teaching them how to draw blueprints and build houses. Just like his big brother, Liam is also handsome and his smile is just as breathtaking.

"Hey Lucas!" I said as I walked up to the porch. Liam looked at me and greeted, and then he turned back to the board. Both kids were focused trying to figure out how to win the game.

"I'm giving Lucas a workout over here playing chess," Liam bragged.

"And here we go again!" Lucas scuffed. His little brother will always make jokes about beating him in these games even when it is clear that Lucas is a better player.

I let out a little laughter, ruffled their hair and promised to be back to play with them, and then I walked into the house.

"Oh, my goodness, thank you Lord, Lola is cooking!" I sighed. I am so hungry. I could see Lola from the foyer that leads to the living room across the open floor layout to the kitchen. She turned around and saw me walking in, "Hey, Danny you are home early."

"Yeah," I said as I eased into a stool at the counter Island, "Since the boys weren't at the community center today, I didn't have to wait for them. Coach Matthew let me speak to the boys today before practice. I think it went well. What time is it anyway?

"It's 4 o'clock. Dinner is almost ready. I'm cooking roast beef tonight with garlic mash potatoes and garlic-spinach, with lemonade."

I instantly started to smile. It was going to be a good night. "So how was your day?" I asked, rubbing my palms gleefully.

"Not bad," she began. She told me that she woke up around 4:45 am and started preparing for work while Evan got the kids set for school. Her clinic was just about ten minutes away, so it was always easy for her to get to work before the start of her shift.

"I called mommy," she added as she started washing off the things she used to cook. "She said you should consider coming back home."

"Back home? Oh, please," I waved that aside.

Mom has always worried about me. She and dad live in a 2-bedroom condominium at the Carolinas Beach area with an Ocean view. They are living their best life over there,

She had told Lola that dad was going in for a job interview at a private gym where he wants to work as an exercise instructor for a few hours. It would keep him in shape and help the seniors stay in shape also.

Mom, on the other hand, loved playing bingo. She is a volunteer at the library, reading books to the children who come in to hear story time. Ben and Grace Mack, our parents, are doing well, but they are all worried about me.

"So how was your day?" Lola asked.

I looked at her and smiled. "You know, sometimes I feel okay, then other times I feel so lost. I wish the military had life coaches that we could see when we leave the military. This could really help to figure out how to cope with the experiences in and out of the military and how to not live in the past that haunts you." I shook my head. I wasn't so sure I wanted to talk about the images of the war which still flashes in my eyes randomly.

"So, how's your GoFundMe page working out?" she asked, sensing that I didn't want to go deep into expressing my worries.

I scuffed. "It's been 3 months, Lola. And all I've got is $25 dollars. $5 dollars that I put in. $10 that Lucas put in, and the other $10 Liam put in. Money that they got from you and Evan." I shook my head again. "I love my family.

"We love you also Danny," she smiled, wiping her hands off on a paper towel.

"I know you all do. I just feel like such a failure. I have no degree. I wanted to start my own business. I figured once I finish college, I would have figured out what business to go into. Now look, my older sister and brother-in-law take care of me. How humiliating for my nephews to see me like this. I wasn't raised to be this way. I fought for my country. I put my life on the line. I stayed up at night so this country could sleep at night. Now, I'm just another veteran without a job. I know I should have hung in there and retired but I mentally couldn't handle it anymore." I paused and took a deep breath. "Lola, I thought about it again."

Lola didn't seem to be listening. "Please help me get out the plates," she said as she got ready to set the table.

"Did you hear me, Lola?" I asked again

"Yeah, I'm listening to you. Just help me get the plates out and set the table. Evan will be home soon and we can all eat together."

"I thought about it again Lola," I repeated. I wanted her to hear me out and not deflect from the topic.

Lola dropped the fork on the floor. "You are scaring me Danny when you start talking like that. I don't know what to do. I can't stand the thought of losing you. I have run out of ways to make you feel wanted and loved. What else can I do to make you feel whole again? Killing yourself is not the answer Danny." She gesticulated with her hands as she voiced out her frustration. "I have been praying for the Holy Spirit to give this family guidance. We need a miracle right now, Oh my God please hear me" she began to cry, and sat down on the floor helplessly. At that moment, I suddenly snapped out my dismal thoughts and realized that I had upset her beyond her control.

I rushed towards her and held her, and then I started to reassure her that I'm okay. It was just a thought. As I wiped the tears in her eyes, Lucas and Liam ran into the kitchen.

"I heard mommy yelling and crying," Liam said, looking at us in confusion. "Is everything okay?"

"Yes, everything is fine," I said, feeling embarrassed that I caused this. "Your mom dropped the fork and tripped on it," I lied.

Lucas walked over to her and whispered into her ears saying, "Mom are you okay?"

Lola got up and touched his face saying, "I am fine, Lucas," and then she waved at Liam to come over. She held them both and kissed their forehead. "Thank you for looking out for me. Can you both start set-ting the table for me."

"Okay," they chorused, looking at both of us suspiciously. They don't seem to believe the story I told. As they set out to fix the table, I got up from the floor feeling more embarrassed and wondering how to talk about what I was feeling without anyone feeling responsible for fixing me. I just wanted to talk to someone.

I resolved that I had to stop upsetting Lola like this. I always feel worse each time I talk to her and see her become so helpless and frustrated. As I wondered how to clear the awkward energy in the air, Evan came in to save the day.

"What's that beautiful smell oozing from the kitchen?" his exciting voice bellowed as he walked into the living room."

"Daddy!" The kids excitedly ran to embrace him. After he kissed them both, he sent them to go and pick up their chess pieces and board from the porch and take them back into their room.

"Baby how was your day today," he asked as he walked up to Lola and gave her a kiss on the lips and a pat on the butt.

"My day went pretty well," Lola smiled at him lovingly, basking in the attention. She started to dish out the food and tell him stories of what happened at the clinic today. She had attended a luncheon that was given for nurses at the community college. One of the speakers, Shirley Bannister came to speak to them from Columbia, South Carolina. She shared stories about her daughter "Demetria" who was a fun third grade school teacher at Windsor elementary, and her husband Dennis Bannister, who cooks and does the grocery shopping.

Having such a husband and daughter was the strong backbone she needed to rise in her career and become the dean of Midland Technical College. So many students have become nurses because of her guidance.

"I remembered her stories because it made me think about my own family," she added.

Evan looked interested, and just like always, he enjoyed listening to her. "So what did you learn today?"

"Well, you know how I complain about the clinic's waiting area when people come in sick to sit and wait to be seen? I always felt like patients should sit in different areas depending on their illness. For example, someone with a cold or flu should sit in a different area from someone who just came in for a check-up. Well, I learned that some clinics use air purifiers with HEPA to keep the air clean of germs and viruses that are in the air. That way, they can keep the air clean so the cold or flu doesn't spread to another patient while sitting in the waiting area to see the doctor. So, I ordered two today for the clinic and two for the house. This way if one person gets a cold the whole house doesn't have to catch the cold.

"Hmm, that's not a bad idea!" Evan chimed in. "I will look into seeing if I can include it into the school air vac system at the school. It could keep down germs and viruses at the school to keep the kids, teachers and staff safe as well."

"So what else did you learn Lola?" I asked.

"Well, Danny, in the black community we have a lot of people that have diabetes," she reduced her voice as if she didn't want anyone else apart from the three of us, to hear this juicy information. "There was one person sitting at my table who was a nurse but she also was into holistic healing. She would share information with patients to add to the doctors' orders. She mentioned that she suggested to a family member that the best way to turn your health around is to juice and take Plantbase iron, berberine, burdock and vitamins for twenty days with the doctor's observation. She also mentioned that she drinks chlorella, spirulina and wheatgrass that she mixes with a glass of water and lemon every morning. She also mentioned Essiac tea to bring down your cholesterol and also treat cancer. She said that she used juicing and exercise to lose twenty-five pounds and it reset her body. She also got rid of the high blood pressure and high cholesterol and diabetes that she suffered. Now she has started eating normal food again, but with more vegetables and less carbs and meat and no sugar. She said, there were two documentaries that changed her life. The first one was "Joe Cross-Fat Sick & Nearly Dead" and the second one was "Jason Vale's Super Juice Me." To sum it all up. I believe for every human illness somewhere in the world there is a plant that will cure it.`

Now Lola looked around and realized that she had made the entire conversation about her day. So, she quickly turned to Evan and asked, "How was your day today, Evan?"

"I see you really had an awesome day, Lola." He said. "I know you will be looking into the things that this nurse shared with everyone today."

She nodded, and then I added, "Yeah, I think I will start looking at those documentaries that she mentioned." They all laughed.

"Well," Evan continued. "The supplies came in for the flooring for the school. We just finished painting all of the walls. It's starting to look like a school. Claremont Hill is really building up the community, and I am so glad I got the contract for the school."

"I'm proud of you babe," Lola said, reaching out to squeeze his hand gently. And then he got to me. "Hey, Danny. How's my brother-in-law doing?"

"Oh Evan," I heaved a sigh. "I'm up and down with emotions."

"Hmm. Any luck with the GoFundMe?"

I shook my head.

"I think I like that idea you have for veterans like yourself. The one where you intend to buy some land and build a camp for the youth. Developing programs for veterans to be mentors in the schools. Teaching the kids about being a team player and about life. Teaching them a trade. Building and making Community centers like franchises like McDonald's. Don't give up. There are a lot of kids that need someone to talk to and feel like someone cares about them. You have to make more people aware of the business of the entrepreneur base camp and mentorship and Community centers that you're trying to start. I know you eventually want to franchise it across the United States everywhere there are veterans and kids who need each other. It's going to happen. We love you, Danny. We may not be able to understand what you are going through but, we are here to help however we can."

I fought hard to keep the tears pooling under my eyelids from drooping. I just nodded, swallowed hard and said "thank you. Uhm, Lola, I didn't mean to upset you today. I have been having those thoughts again and I just needed to talk to someone and I shared it with Lola and it really upset her." Then Evan looked at Lola and asked if she was okay. "Yes, I'm fine," she replied, looking unbothered. "I just don't know what to say to fix how Danny is feeling."

"Danny, if you need someone to talk to and you're feeling discouraged or feel like giving up then please call me and not Lola. I don't need her to have a nervous breakdown. She runs this family and we all need her. Some things are just too heavy for her to lift. Give it to me instead. I do the heavy lifting for this family."

"I'm sorry. Of course," I said, feeling blessed to have them in my life.

"Where are you, boys?" he called out to the kids who had gone out to bring their chess pieces inside.

"We're coming!" They echoed back, and within a few minutes, we were all gathered around the table eating the sumptuous dinner and sharing light-hearted conversations.

Malik's Barbershop

I woke to the piercing sound of my alarm.

It was seven-thirty A.M. on my cell which meant the clatter I heard came from Evan preparing the boys for school. As I lay there, I thought about how to raise money for a business that would employ veterans who had no jobs to work with the youth. After several minutes, I sprang out of bed, intensely grateful that there were three bathrooms in the house. I wouldn't be in anyone's way as I got ready.

"Let's do this!" I told myself in the bathroom mirror.

As I walked out of the house, everyone was gone. The sun shone bright on the brisk winter day in December. Christmas was in the air. Houses were decorated for the season and my steps felt light as I headed out to my part time job at the barber shop where I got my haircut. A ghost of a smile quirked my lips as I remembered the few soldiers I gave haircuts when I was in the military.

"Hey Mack," they would call, "I need a shape up."

I never specifically learned anywhere, I just seemed to have a knack for it. Since the fellows on the base were happy with the cuts, I found a shop and the owner rented a chair to me for half a day while the guy who normally has the chair is getting his degree in business. The chair pays for itself and puts a few hundred dollars in my pocket from time to time, so I could contribute to the house. Evan and Lola take the money because they know I would feel worse about myself if they didn't. It also puts gas in my car and pays for my car insurance. Thank goodness, my car was paid off by the time I got out of the army, I did something right.

My search for a better job had been hopeless, Malik's place was a blessing. Thank God for Malik, another brother who was there for me. Coach Matthew and Malik gave me a chance to prove myself. They saw the value in me that I had not seen in myself. It's funny how we start to see ourselves through other people's eyes and we forget we ourselves define who we are. People thought that there was no help in the hood. They were so wrong. Not everyone in the hood is out for themselves.

"Good morning," I greeted the people I came across as I walked into the shop. It had blond hardwood floors with a 3D floor mural that appeared like the floor had an enormous hole in it and almost convinced a person that they could fall through.

It freaked me out every time. I imagined that was the precise reason why Malik put it there. To scare people when they looked down. He did watch for their reactions and laughed raucously when they fell for it.

On one wall, where the couch and table and chairs rested, people played checkers as they awaited their turn. There is a 3D mural of a boardwalk with the sun shining and palm trees and sand with the ocean in the background. Malik never took a vacation, he figured he would have his vacation come to him. It was pretty nice, except for the freaky, hell's gate floor. *That* was surreal.

Inside, a 3D beach and ocean mural was on the side of the wall which was also a waiting section with chairs and tables. There, people could buy products to shave with, to keep the face tight. That section also held a coffee machine, soda machine, snack machine and ATM. The barbershop sold blue t-shirts and sweatshirts with the inscription, *shape up at Malik's barber shop* with a picture of clippers on it and the address, phone number in white.

Malik, the owner, looked up from cutting a guy's hair, tossed a toothy smile at me.

"Good morning. How's a brother doing today?" he asked.

"I'm okay," I replied with an answering smile. Then, I started to set up. A young man walked in and sat by the murals and waited for me to finish.

"Okay, young king come on over and have a seat." I motioned at the leather chair, "your fade needs a touch up?"

"Yeah," he replied.

"I got you."

It was 8:45 A.M. and Steve Harvey was on the radio talking smack. I asked for people's opinions. I caught the first part of the strawberry letter segment, in my car.

"Yeah," said Malik. "The brother always has something interesting to say about people's stories that they write in need of advice. It's always so nice to hear a brother trying to uplift the culture." Silence descended among us, as we listened to the news and music on the radio. Six heads later it was midday. The other guy Don just breezed into the shop with a big smile on his face. Purposely, he averted his gaze from the floor. He laughed because he knew people were watching for his reaction.

"What's up everybody!" he boomed. He walked over and fist bumped Malik and me and the other guys in the shop. Don's shift began at 1P.M. and mine was rounding up so I could give the chair to him. Since we shared the space, we each paid half the rent. That way, it reduced our load and Malik was able to pay his bills which kept the shop going.

The other three guys that paid for their chair were full timers and they had been there for at least five years.

Malik was a pillar in the community. He offered haircuts to the homeless on days when business was slow. He brought sandwiches to the shop just in case his crew was hungry and we didn't make much money that day to buy lunch.

Malik's father was in the military so he understood that life. When he heard I just got out of the army and was looking for a workspace, he scooped me right up, talked to Don about sharing a chair. This was Don's last semester in college. It was not easy to combine his education with work. He lived within the school's campus and that relieved him of bills. He still has to tackle student loans though.

"Well, that's it," I said, as I dusted the specks of hair from the customer's neck.

The customer inspected my work and grinned at his reflection. "That's what's up!" he got up. "Thanks my man," he said and slipped me some cash including a tip.

"Not a problem," I said with a pleased smile. To Don, I said, "I'm getting out of your way."

Don flashed that silly grin, "no worries."

I packed up my tools just in time as Don's customer waltzed into the shop.

"What's up everybody?" He, too, avoided the chasm below. The first time he came to the shop to get a trim he'd screamed bloody murder, held his arms out to try to hold on to anything so he wouldn't fall. Halted conversations had immediately changed to booming laughter.

A chorus of "What's up," trailed his greeting.

I approached the exit as Don settled his customer in. "See ya'll later," I called out.

"Later man," most of the guys replied.

Malik yelled "I'll see you tomorrow."

"Right on," I replied.

They call me "G"

As I hopped into my car, I decided to go for lunch at my friend Sam's job. He worked at Claremont Hill hotel. We always treated ourselves on Friday at the fancy restaurant inside the hotel.

As I made it into the hotel's swarming entrance, I dialed Sam's phone. "Yo, I'm here. Where are you at?"

"Aw man, I'm running late. I'm finishing up with a couple who's looking for a venue to have their wedding and reception here. Wait at the lobby, I'll be there in thirty minutes."

"Yeah, okay," I replied, not the least bit disappointed. Sam was almost always busy. I found a seat at the lobby and went to take it. A blond-haired, blue-eyed Ken doll, in a suit, moved over on the couch so I couldn't sit there. He had a familiar expression I knew meant he didn't want me sitting there. He looked at me then, turned away and continued with his phone conversation. My blood heated. This was the kind of shit that drove me crazy. *Asshole,* I mumbled under my breath fighting to control my breathing with deep inhales. Suppressing the obvious disrespect, I left the lobby and headed to the restaurant.

As I waited to be seated, a woman with a business suit walked in, eyed my casual outfit and said, "I need a table."

Still riled from the other encounter, I gave a gruff reply, "I don't work here." She huffed out a frustrated breath and stretched her pearl-clad neck in search of a waiter. My curiosity was piqued though, I wondered why she assumed I worked here. I was clad in blue jeans and a fitted black sweater with a wool jacket over it. Nothing close to the tuxedos the waiters wore.

The maître D' came to us, in his haughty black tux and asked out loud "how many will be in your party?"

The lady, who now regarded me with some suspicion, replied, "just me."

He swiveled on his glossy Italian shoes, "follow me."

"Uh, I was here first." I said.

The maître D' paused mid-step, "I'll be right back."

I fought to reel in an outpour of protests and annoyance, when a man who stood behind me muttered, "I hate when that happens." I turned to meet his pitying gaze, "Hi, I saw what just happened. Are you here by yourself?"

I glanced around to ascertain that the handsome, slightly taller, African American spoke to me. He gave a crooked smile and awaited my response.

I snapped out of it and focused, "yes, for now anyway. Killing time for...twenty-five minutes." "Would you have lunch with me, please? Twenty-five minutes is enough." he inquired with a beguiling smile and a tiny quirk to his eyebrows.

I was thrown aback by his kind understanding in his eyes. Before I realized it, I'd accepted the invite. The maître D' returned.

"How many are in your party?"

The nice man replied, "two."

"Follow me" said the maître D'.

"This is my first time here, are you also visiting?" he asked as we were seated.

"Nah," I answered, "I have a friend that works here," I replied with an unconscious vagueness.

"Are you ok?"

"Well, to tell you the truth, not really." Now, I thought, I would never see him again. I could just unload on him. I needed someone to talk to before these thoughts of punching somebody reared its head.

"You can talk to me. Seems like you got a lot more going on than the crappy service?"

I opened my mouth, but the waiter interrupted with a cheery, "Hello, I'm Scott your server. Can I get you something to drink? We have a wonderful selection of wine."

The guy glanced at me, nodded for me to go first, "Ah, yes I'll just have some water with lemon." Scott beamed at the man, "and you sir."

"I'll have the same, thank you."

"Alright, here's the menu. I will be back to take your order."

"Thank you." I said.

"Back to you," he said.

I peered down at my watch; Ten minutes had gone by. "I was just going to say...that uh," I swallowed, "I have been depressed and angry lately and sometimes, things just trigger it."

"I'm sorry to hear that. What have you been depressed about?" he asked, leaning forward, concern etched in his features.

"Well, I graduated from high school and got into college then 9/11 happened. My roommate's mom was there and she never came home. From listening to his stories and hearing him cry at night just about killed me. Then when it was time for our sophomore year to return back to college he didn't come back. Suicide attempt. I was so enraged that I joined the Army."

"My parents were in a daze because I did it so fast that they didn't have a chance to talk me out of it. I did four years and I had two tours in Afghanistan. The risks started to tell on me and I had to get out."

"On my last trip I was talking to a soldier friend of mine. We were walking and he got shot right beside me. The blast stunned and rooted me to the spot. Then someone made a grab at me, amidst the shower of bullets. I keep asking why it wasn't me? Maybe if I hadn't moved he would still be alive? One time I even had a dream about him telling me he was okay but I still find myself recreating that day over and over, reconstructing an instance where I could have done something to save him."

"I'm out of the military now and I can't find a job. I've been getting one rejection after another. I'm starting to feel like a failure and most times, I just wanna give up."

Scott, the waiter arrived with our beverages, shutting off my outpour. "Are you ready to order?" I lowered my head, belatedly embarrassed by my whining and vulnerability. I heard the guy place his order. I raised my head long enough to rattle the commonest dish I could remember since I'd not taken a glance at the menu.

"Coming right up," says the waiter.

The nice man began to speak, "I heard a story about a woman who came to Jesus and said, I had a dream last night and you were in it. Then she looked at him closely and asked Jesus, 'were you there?' Jesus replied, 'When you dream, that's when the spirit world connects with the physical world.'

He smiled and added, "I don't know if that really happened but, I do know that Matthew 2:13 in the bible says that God's angel spoke to Joseph in a dream telling him to arise and take Mary and the baby to Egypt. Genesis 28:10-22 speaks of Jacob seeing God's Angels and hearing from God in his dreams and in Matthew 1:20 speaks of one of God's angels speaking to Joseph in a dream about Mary being with child and it was okay to marry her. So maybe, your friend is perfectly fine..

I didn't know much about the Scriptures, but his words drove me to think. I wondered if there really was a connection, and if he was all right.

The man cut into my musing, "you said you have been getting rejection after rejection and because of that you feel like a failure. I'd like to tell you a story about a daughter who complained to her father about her struggles. She was tired of fighting also. It just seemed like when one problem was solved another problem was on its way. She just wanted to give up on life. Her father was a chef and he took her to the kitchen. He filled three pots with water and put them on a high flame. Then he placed potatoes in one pot, in the second pot he put eggs in, and in the third pot he put coffee beans.

"Then, he sat and let the water boil without saying a word to his daughter. The daughter impatiently waited, wondering what he was doing. After twenty minutes he turned the burners off. Then he took the potatoes and put them in a bowl. He placed the eggs in another bowl. Then, he poured the coffee out into a cup and put them all on a table. Turning to his daughter he asked her 'what do you see?'

'Potatoes, eggs and coffee,' she replied fast. The father said, 'look closer and touch the potatoes.' She did and noticed the potatoes had gone soft. Then he asked her to crack the eggs."

"After peeling off the shell she noticed it was a hard-boiled egg. Finally, he asked her to sip the coffee. Its rich aroma puts a smile on her face."

'Father, what does this mean?' she asked. He explained that the potatoes, the eggs and the coffee beans had faced the same adversity, 'the boiling water.' However, each one reacted differently."

"The potato went in strong, hard and unrelenting, but, in boiling water it became soft and weak.

The egg was fragile with the thin outer shell protecting its liquids interior until it was put in the boiling water. Then the inside of the egg became hard."

"However, the ground coffee beans were unique. After they were exposed to the same boiling water they changed the water and created something new that smelled and tasted good.

The same boiling water that softens the potatoes hardens the eggs but the boiling water changes the coffee beans into coffee. Then looking at his daughter he asked, 'which one are you?'"

I was transfixed by his calming baritone as he continued.

"You see, boiling water represents the struggles that we all deal with in life. You can deal with the struggle like the potato goes in hard and strong but, over time the struggle wears you out and you become soft, weak and powerless."

You deal with the struggle like the egg by being fragile, vulnerable but over time when the struggle becomes too much you become hard and distant with people."

"Or you could deal with the struggle like the coffee bean that changed the water into something better."

"You can become flexible and adapt to the new situation or environment to overcome the obstacle. Like taking a Lemon and turning it into lemonade. When you are faced with a struggle, you have choices, so choose wisely."

The nice man concluded and met my eyes, "now that you are out of the Army, how do you want to deal with your struggle?"

I had never looked at life like that before. I was rendered speechless. This was a new concept and a whole new way of thinking for me.

The nice man continued, "in life things happen around us, things happen to us, but the only thing that truly matters is how you choose to react to them and what you make out of it. Life is all about learning, adapting and converting all of the struggles that we experience into something positive like the coffee bean turning into a wonderful smelling aroma and tasteful."

"There were a lot of soldiers that were killed while you were in Afghanistan, but you focus on the one that was talking to you. The guilt of surviving is not your burden, like all of the soldiers who came home alive from Afghanistan is not your victory."

Just sitting there I'd gotten so engrossed in the lecture I looked down and didn't realize that my meal had been served. He'd managed to topple my previous perception. The first blooms of hope and value surged through me.

I looked at this nice man and said, "thank you. You understand me and my struggle."

Tears prickled at the back of my eyes. I could see how he looked at me like he could see a light inside me. I struggled to speak through the wedge in my throat, I could not let those tears drop.

"I'm sorry for unloading on you like that and you don't even know my name. I'm Danny." It was crazy how we met. I forgot to introduce myself to you. I'm so glad I sat down to have lunch with you. I feel lighter. Like a heavy weight has been lifted off my chest."

"What's your name?" I asked him.

"They call me 'G'." he replied, eying me like I was an interesting person. He added, "I came here to look for a guy named Danny Mack? Do you know him?"

My heart did a double flip, "Uh, yeah, why are you looking for him?

"My girlfriend Joy knows that I am interested in investing in people. She got me started by looking at the *Go fund me* website, and I read his story and I came here to see him and how we could help each other."

I was frozen with surprise, G, passed a curious glance at me. "Are you okay?"

I shook my head with excitement, "I am Danny Mack." G stared at me mystified, how could it be? What were the odds?

He shook his head in disbelief, smiled at me and said, "Look at God."

After lunch we continued to talk. We walked out of the restaurant into the lobby of the hotel.

"I really enjoyed having lunch with you and I am looking forward to meeting with you tomorrow before you leave.

I really want you to meet my family," I said with happiness.

"I look forward to it Danny."

We did the one-armed, slap on the back hug then I left for my car. I looked back and saw G head towards the elevators. Behind the wheel I realized that I left without having lunch with Sam.

"Oh boy," I muttered and dialed Sam.

"Hey Sam."

"Danny, hi. Listen, I'm sorry for keeping you waiting. The couple had so many questions about prices. I showed them some rooms where they and their guests would stay. How can I make it up to you Danny? Don't worry about it, Sam. I can't wait to tell you what happened at lunch at your hotel, while I was waiting for you. I hope it was good Danny, because I worked through lunch. Trust me. It was good Sam. I have to go to the community center and meet my nephews there. You know Sam, I hang out with my nephews and volunteer there until their chess class is over. Then we go home. Yeah, I know. Call me later so we can catch up Danny.

Basketball & Entrepreneurs

I got out of my car and walked over to the community center. I felt taller than when I left yesterday. I peeked into one of the rooms where the kids learn to play chess. I saw Lucas and Liam playing as I breathed easy. I decided to head to the gym where they knew to meet me after.

"Hello," I greeted Coach Matthew in his office.

"Hello Danny. The boys really enjoyed your talk with them yesterday and so did I."

"Thank you for the opportunity coach," I replied with a grin. Coach Matthew stares out the window that faces the gym, at the kids practicing. Then he directed his piercing gaze at me.

"Do you want to go out there and give them a few words before I get started?"

"Yes, I would love that Coach."

I opened his office door and stepped out to the gymnasium.

"Hello, guys!" I hollered. The boys paused from throwing hoops.

"Hey, Mr. Mack," most of them chorused.

"Come on over to the bleachers fellas. I just want to talk to you for a few minutes before practice starts."

The boys rushed over and took a seat on the bleachers, turning avid attention to me.

"Thank you boys," I said, eager to share my thoughts.

"Ok, Mr. Mack what you got on your mind?" a kid in front asked.

"Well, I was thinking about the conversation we had yesterday about your dreams of getting rich."

"Oh yeah, yeah, yeah," the young kings shouted.

"Well, everything is built on sales," I started, "the clothes you wear. The food you eat. Where you live. This Community Center. The bleachers that you're seating on. But, first I want you to understand there is no job loyalty. Meaning you can work for a company and they can go out of business and you will be without a job. But, if I share with you the importance of sales and having your own business. To serve people with a smile and tell them you're thankful when they buy from you because people love to be appreciated when they spend their money. So I came up with an idea for how you'd all make money."

"Wow, Mr. Mack. Was it?" Another kid asked.

"We will inscribe a motivating quote on a wrist band. The message on the wrist band will remind people they can win and that is one way of helping someone who really needs inspiration. The more people you serve the more money you will make. So, introduce yourself with a smile to someone new everyday"

"That sounds great Mr. Mack. Do we need money?"

"Yes, you will need money. But what I will do is I will be the lender. What that means is I will buy the product. You sell. When I get my money back. Then we can split the profit. So, if one person sells ten wrist bands, we share fifty-fifty. Then each person has to buy more wristbands from your profit to stay in business. I'm going to buy wristbands that will say, ' Have faith, The best revenge is success, Trust your gut' and I want you young kings to wear it yourself and sell them too."

"Then we will see who makes the most money in a week after you get the wristbands. Whoever wins by making the most money gets a $10 gift card to a place you like to eat. You will set your own price. My goal is to help you develop the mindset to become rich. What do you guys think?" "I'm down Mr. Mack."

"Me too."

"We are all down with that Mr. Mack."

"Great, I will order the wrist bands and make sure you start selling them to family, friends. Then you will be entrepreneurs."

"What's that Mr. Mack?"

"It means you become the boss of your own business."

"Oh yeah, I like that Mr. Mack."

My smile bloomed, looking at all of the young kings. I felt like we were starting to connect. I turned and noticed Coach Matthew was listening and he smiled at me as I said, "I'm finished Coach. Standing next to the coach were Lucas and Liam. They wore proud smiles.

"That's my uncle," they told the team members that listened. The boys started to clap, joining Lucas and Liam. The entire atmosphere moved me. Finally, I felt that my nephews saw the value in me I didn't even know I possessed. I was dignified and respected. It was good to give my time and try to teach the young kings there was more than one way to win.

"Come on boys, let's go home and see what your mother is cooking." I gave my nephews a high five and waved goodbye at everyone in the gym.

A New Beginning

Pulling up in front of the house I could see the lights on at the porch. It is amazing how Lola has white lights round the front yard, all along the framed roof and railings of the porch. She has them wrapped around the chain of the swings and at the door also. She has a tan doormat that reads in black print, *The magic of Christmas is not in the presents, but in His Presence.* Her positive energy all over the place. I got out of the car, thinking, *I feel hopeful, I feel like I can make a difference. I matter. I have something people need. Love, knowledge, and my story. Thank you Father God for blessing me by letting me see the battle was in my mind the whole time and that's why nobody could see what I was going*

through but you God.

Walking into the house with Lucas and Liam I could perceive dinner. Evan and Lola were setting the table.

"Oh, Danny, great. You guys are home. We were just getting ready to wait to have dinner. Everyone's plate is already on the table. Come on in, wash up and have dinner," said Lola.

"Thank you Lola."

"Thanks mom. Hi dad," the boys greeted happily as they went to put their back packs down and wash their hands.

"How is everyone doing today?" I asked.

"Ok," Lola said.

"Fine" replied Evan. "Danny, I'm so glad you're home. We started putting the floors down in the school today. I was just telling Lola. I would love for you to stop by and take a look.

"Sure thing, Evan." I accepted with a shrug.

Lola and Evan paused, setting down dishes and stared wide-eyed at me, "you would?" Evan asked, making sure he'd heard right. I couldn't blame them.

"Yes, I know I have not shown much interest with the school project you're working on Evan. I just could not see anything but my failures. Like a person with a tooth ache all they can think about is the pain they are in. They can't see anything else. Once the pain is gone you can focus on other things again. I just couldn't figure out how to overcome this negative energy so; I could be a part of something positive and productive. I felt stuck. Replaying the same story over and over like it would get better each time. They call that insanity right?" I laughed as I dried my hands after washing them in the kitchen sink and sat down to have dinner. The boys joined my side.

Evan and Lola laughed; a sound filled with relief.

"How was your day today Danny?"

"I love you so much Lola for cooking dinner." I complimented as I dug in. I savored the tastiness with my eyes closed, before answering.

"I had the craziest and amazing day ever!"

"Really?" said Evan.

"Tell us Danny. What happened? Lola joined. Liam and Lucas looked on.

I dropped my spoon and related the event at the hotel, almost word for word.

"To cut the long story short," I concluded, "the conversation that I had with this guy was so insightful I felt like he knew me. It was like someone asked the Holy Spirit to give me guidance and the Holy Spirit sent this guy. Lola smiled and exchanged glances with Evan then back at me with curiosity.

"I don't know if it was his delivery or his sincerity but his message went straight to my heart. He allowed me to shift my way of thinking about how I saw myself and my struggles. I realized I had options. I can change the play in the middle of the game. Now, I understand when the bible says, "transform your mind."

"On the way home I thought about Dave Chappelle working hard on his show. Finally, he got an unbelievable offer and he changed the play in the middle of the game. He had the foresight to see danger in the middle of a 50 million dollar offer. All his fans saw was a lot of money he walked away from but, he looked deeper than that and he saw his dignity, integrity and the respect that he commanded from those in charge would be compromised and that weighed more than gold to him I bet. It's just a different way of thinking."

"He realized he had choices. He stepped away from the people, places and things that were enticing to him, to keep his mind right. You have to put respect on his name.

He's a black king that we can admire and follow his play if necessary. It's crazy when I sit back and think about it because we as black people want to be respected."

" Anyway, come to find out the guy from lunch is from a place outside of Fayetteville, North Carolina. He came to Claremont Hill looking for this guy to help that he found on the *Go Fund Me* site."

"Wow," said Lola.

"That's fantastic!" Evan had stopped eating to focus on me.

"I wonder who the person is," said Lola.

I looked at Lola with excitement. "The person's name was Danny Mack."

Evan dropped his fork and Lola's voice rose, "What? What? What?!! Was it you?! Danny, was it you?" Lola stood. Liam and Lucas laughed at their parents' reactions.

"Yes! It was me!"

"I can't believe it!" exclaimed Lola.

"So how does he want to help you," Evan asked.

"Well, you will find out tomorrow because he will be here to meet you all and we will discuss what he had in mind."

"No way!" said Lola.

"Wow," said Evan.

"Thank you Lola for telling me to put that I need help on *Go Fund Me.* I thought I was just wasting my time."

"Well, how did things go at the community center today?" Lola inquired.

Lucas jumped. "Uncle Danny spoke to the basketball team mom and no one said a word. All eyes were on him."

Then Liam chimed in. "Yes, he spoke and we all listened. He talked about starting a business to help the team make money. I noticed how they reacted while listening to our Uncle."

Lucas cut in, "yeah, I could see that they were really interested in what uncle Danny was saying. We felt so proud of him."

Lola and Evan looked quite impressed. "You had an awesome day, uh Danny."

I beamed, "yes, I did." We continued with dinner after that while the kids told us about their day.

* * *

Saturday afternoon and Lola was in the kitchen preparing lunch. G would arrive soon. I was a bag of jumpy nerves. Evan was in the kitchen talking to Lola about how excited he was for me. I overheard them as I passed by the kitchen a few minutes ago and I have Liam and Lucas with me in my bedroom telling me what shirt and pants to wear.

"No jeans, Uncle Danny."

"Yes, jeans are fine," said Lucas.

"I have changed twice listening to you guys," I said frustrated. "Okay, let's all agree on something."

"Okay," Liam agreed, "wear the jeans."

"No, don't wear the jeans," said Lucas.

"Liam's right, wear the pants." Liam smiled and said,

"Okay I can agree with Lucas."

I just shook my head smiling and said "that's why I love you guys so much. You make me laugh. Pants it is!"

The lasagna and garlic bread was almost ready for lunch and Lola's special chocolate icing vanilla cake for dessert sat on the island in her favorite glass cake holder with the glass lid and flowers, next to them. She always makes things special.

"The doorbell! Liam and Lucas shouted.

"I got it," I said, trudging to the door. I opened it with excitement without asking who was at the door. "G!"

"Hi Danny."

"It's good to see you again. How are you? Come on in, let's get you out of the cold. My family has been anxious to meet you. Have a seat."

"Oh, yes. Thank you.

"Lola and Evan, G is here," I called. Lola and Evan come out to meet G. Then Liam and Lucas join.

"Hello," Lola and Evan greeted.

"Hi," Liam and Lucas piped up.

"G, this is my sister Lola she is a nurse and her husband Evan who owns a general contracting business. My nephews Liam and Lucas.

"Hello, family" smiling, G returned their greetings. "Did Danny tell you how we met?"

"Yes," said Lola, smiling. "It was meant to be."

"I think so, Lola," G agreed.

"Well," said Lola, "we will let you talk and lunch will be served in an hour. Is that okay with both of you?"

"Yes," said G. "I love a home cooked meal." They all shuffled from the room.

"Are you sure you don't want something to drink?" I said, ready to serve.

"No, I'm good for now."

"Okay," I said, "I don't know where to begin."

"Well," G said, "let's start with my agenda and then you tell me yours and hopefully we can work together to make it happen."

"I will start," said G. "I was a teacher in Jersey City at Peace elementary school. Then I relocated to a place outside of Fayetteville, North Carolina. I am starting a camp there and I would like someone like you to be a part of it. From what I read about you on *Go Fund Me.* You are a veteran and you came home and couldn't find work. You would help your sister out by picking up your nephews from the community center. It's by helping out your sister with the boys. Are you volunteering by any chance?"

"Yes I just started helping the basketball coach there." I said, like a kid who got the right answer in class.

"You also work at a barbershop part-time.

"Yes."

G continued, "I want to help inner city kids find a sense of peace and learn about different career paths. I think having a strong male presence around would give them an example of what it looks like to be a man. They can hear your story and other veteran stories. I believe this would build a bridge between you and the kids. I don't have it all put together. I think with your ideas and my backing our dream can come true. What do you think?"

I just shook my head in disbelief. "G, one minute I'm feeling hopeless about my future and the next minute I'm feeling hopeful about my future. I didn't see this for my future but after coming out of the Army the only skill I had that was self-taught was cutting hair."

"I was so caught up with rejections that I didn't know how I could get a job with no degree and not having an idea of what I wanted to do. I knew I wanted to be an entrepreneur and since going to the Community Center I started seeing myself in these kids. I want to start a program that would bring veterans and the inner-city children together. I would like to teach them about business. I would like to build up their self-esteem. I would like for the kids to look back one day and say it's because I was a part of Mr. Mack's program that I am successful today. I would like to help my fellow veterans who need work and would like to work with the inner-city kids. I wanted to franchise community centers for all inner cities that need one. I want to buy some land and build a camp for the kids to get out of the city for a while and replenish themselves and learn a trade."

G listened to me intently. "I would like for you to come visit me in the next few days so we can start putting something together and I want you to see where I want the camp," said G.

"It would be my pleasure," I returned. "I could come for just a couple of days. I have to get back to work and to be here for my nephews."

"It will only take a couple of days to see the area and we can implement your curriculum on the campgrounds. The camp will be finished by the spring. It would also be great for your nephews to be there for the summer. I know that would help out your family and the boys would love it," he said.

"Danny, I also want to give you $100,000 for you to get what you need to start your program and hire a couple of people to get it started. The program will last for the summer. I have a team that can help you with the proper paperwork and guidance you will need to get your program started. I'll also pay you for coming out for these couple of days because I know you'll be missing work. Here Danny, this is $5,000 cash in this envelope and your ticket coming and going will be covered. Just go to the train station on the days you pick and the tickets will be paid for. We need each other."

I stared in shock at him. Tears prickled the back of my eyes and before I could hold back, it streamed down my cheeks. We shook hands and I managed a croaky, "thank you, you have given me a beautiful gift. You have given me hope, respect and my dignity back. Thank you. God bless you." I reached for a tissue on the coffee table and wiped my eyes.

"Let's eat," I said to G. I know you have to be back on your way home."

"I can't wait to get started."

"Yo!" I yelled out, "Lola, we're hungry."

Lola came out and called for her kids too. Evan joined. I asked, "what can I do to help Lola?"

"You can put in the garlic bread now."

"Good, said Evan, "I'm hungry

Who is G?

"Next stop is Fayetteville," the conductor announced and interrupted my sleep. I glanced around to make sure I had everything. I gazed out of the window feeling the peacefulness and listening to the rumbling wheels.

This was when I took a break from the stress of life. Moments like this, I get replenishment and feel connected to God. I was able to let go of my troubles, relax and keep functioning. Thirty minutes went by, "Fayetteville," announced the train conductor. The train pulled into the Fayetteville station. It was a sunny day sixty degrees and Christmas was a couple of weeks away.

In Jersey City, it was about forty degrees and I was not missing the cold. The train came to a stop and I got in the line to get off of the train. On the last step, I spotted Joy, my girlfriend.

A smile graced my face. I strode toward her, dropped my bags and enveloped her soft body in my arms. Our kiss lasted for seconds but felt like an hour. Love for her poured from me. I'd missed everything about her.

"I prayed last night and thanked God for you. Thank you baby for surprising me by being here to pick me up from the train. I missed your voice, so talk to me," I said.

I saw an answering love in her eyes, "G, thank you, for making me feel like my happiness is your priority and, there is nothing more irreplaceable than your happiness to me," she gushed.

"I missed you and I wanted to surprise you, G." she said.

I smiled and picked up my bags feeling like the luckiest man alive. I told Chip, I would pick you up from the train so he didn't have to come," she continued.

"What's going on, love?" I asked, as we approached the car.

"I was thinking last night, it has been three years now and we are still together. I was honestly afraid that with all of your money and the things that you have accomplished that you would have moved on to a big city and found someone else that's glamorous and high maintenance but, you are still here. I just wonder why?"

G stopped walking and put his bags down and pulled Joy close to him.

"Joy, I came from the big city and I have dated beautiful looking women that made a lot of money and kept themselves together, but, for me, I felt that their priorities were different from mine. What was on top of my list was on the bottom of theirs. I feel like you and my priorities align and we share the same values. My agenda since I've been here is to create an environment where black people could flourish. You have poured into me, a way for me to make that happen through your vision. I had the means and you had the vision that allowed me to see how I could make a difference which has always been my goal. I knew what I wanted but I didn't see how I could achieve it."

"You have given Maya, your best friend, a job and encouraged her to thrive in the projects that she has developed for the kids to become entrepreneurs. You have been a solid foundation for all of us. Where am I going babe? No other woman has brought out in me this sense of accomplishment. I want to give you back the same feelings that you have given me. I want your cup to overflow with love from me. You deserve that and more."

"Thank you G, for those kind words and for allowing me to be the strong woman that I am and not make me feel that I have to decrease so that you can increase."

"No, baby girl, your personality doesn't intimidate me, it illuminates me. I have watched you G and how you handle yourself when things get overwhelming. I don't know where you get your confidence from but it's exhilarating. Even when you make a mistake you are able to pivot and turn the whole situation around to make it work. I admire that about you and that makes me trust you with my love and your guidance. You make it easy for me to allow you to lead in this relationship. You respect my opinions and I respect yours," I pressed my lips gently to hers, winked at her then picked up my bags.

Joy said, "I also want you to know that I've been busy renting out your houses and helping Maya prepare for her Winter Blessings Fair. Chip and Larry have been helping the vendors with showing where to put their booths so they can set up all along Black Wall Street, for the fair. There will be heat lamps for vendors and shoppers to stay warm while shopping. Since the first fair was such a success. Maya has many vendors that are a part of the fair now. We have raised close to five-hundred thousand dollars in ads and vendors are still signing up to be a part of it. That is not including the hotel reservations."

At the car, I set my bags in the trunk and sat on the passenger's side of Joy's car. She drove off. "So, how was your trip?"

"Very interesting." I paused, "I found Danny. We met at the restaurant in my hotel. It was crazy." I related every detail that happened on my trip with Danny. "When you have trained for war and, then you go to war and, you get to come back home alive from war. You have a story to tell and there are a lot of people that need to hear his story and other veterans stories. These conversations can shape our culture in a positive way. Seeing life through the eyes of our veterans. Learning about what it takes to be a hero and *shero*. Changing the narrative of how people see our veterans," I said.

"Well, I can't wait to meet Danny," Joy intoned. "I'm so excited for you to see how much work we have done preparing for the Winter Festival. I picked up your mom and sisters from the airport last night and they are staying at your house. They are very excited about the festival. We'll be going out to dinner tonight. My mom will be there too. Larry and Chip have picked the place and taken care of the reservations to where we are going to eat tonight. So I guess you and I will be surprised together.

I smiled and said, "being surprised is not a bad thing."

"I guess so. I'm just used to taking care of things like that. I told them that I and Maya would take care of it but Larry and Chip insisted they'd do it. I'm almost finished with my Christmas shopping. I brought some beautiful bracelets with uplifting messages and beads on them as grab bag gifts. Do you feel like wrapping gifts with me tomorrow night? We'll have fun and you can help me with your mom and sisters bake some chocolate chip cookies. We'll be kinda busy with the winter festival in the next couple of days. I'm looking forward to it and I love the gospel music concert on the last night of the festival."

She bounced excitedly, "your mom and sisters with my mom, Maya and her mom and myself we'll have a ball."

I chuckled, "I can see. Just let me know when you want to wrap gifts. You always make things fun, Joy. You will find a way to make a game out of anything. You help me clean the house and you will make a game out of it." We shared a laugh.

"What are you wearing tonight?" said Joy,

"Jeans and a black sweater," I answered.

"Hmm, maybe I will wear a pair of jeans also."

Pulling up into my driveway. Joy said, "I'm going home to get ready for tonight. I will see later." "Okay. I guess Larry and Chip will let us know where we are going soon."

I gave Joy a passionate kiss, touched her on her nose and winked then got out of the car. "I'll see you tonight Joy."

"Okay," Joy replied.

I waved at her as Joy drove out. When I got into the house, I brought my travel bag upstairs. No one was around, I guessed they were at Chips house. The phone rang. It was Larry.

"Hello Larry."

"Hey G. I'm on my way to pick up Jesse from the airport. He's going to stay at my house. We'll meet up with you later for dinner."

"That sounds good. I'll see you guys."

I dropped the call, took a quick shower and grabbed a quick, needed shuteye.

* * *

Larry got to the airport and checked his phone for time. *Oh, good I'm right on time.* Jesse's flight would land in a few minutes. Larry sat to wait. A few minutes went by and he spotted people getting off the plane. He looked anxiously for Jesse trying not to miss him at the gate. Jesse saw Larry and called,

"Hey."

Larry saw Jesse and he called back

"Hey," smiling from ear to ear. They give each other a warm embrace.

"How was your flight?" asked Larry.

"It was really nice. We didn't hit any air pockets, it was a smooth flight. What's up Larry? How are you? You look good. I haven't seen you guys since the summer."

As they walked to get Jesse's suitcases Larry started to fill Jesse in. "I don't know man. I have no reason to complain. What about you Jesse?"

"Well, it's the same old same old thing. I go to work. I'm trying to find ways to get the kids excited about their vision, where they see themselves going. Some of them are focused and most of them don't see the importance but I'm hanging in there. My bills are getting paid. I'm dating but no one is special yet. I finally closed on the house that I was telling you about. I'm feeling really good about myself but, I'm feeling like I'm missing out. You guys are doing big things down here. I'm still in the same place in life when you left and you guys are doing big things down here. I feel like I'm stagnant." Jesse picked his luggage up from the conveyor belt and they continued toward Larry's car.

Jesse continued, "I think I might have lost sight of my dream or maybe I need a dream. I have so much more to give but I'm so busy not wanting to rock the boat. I stay in my comfort zone so that I don't explore other opportunities to expand and grow."

At Larry's car, Jesse placed his luggage in the trunk. They got into the car. "I understand what you are talking about Jesse," said Larry. "I have kind of gotten lost myself. I have plenty of money. More money than I ever have had before. I live in the house that G built for me. I have been working with Joy and Maya with renting out the houses and managing them that G is building. Don't get me wrong. I enjoy what I'm doing. I get paid more than what I was making in Jersey but I feel like I have gotten lost."

"I couldn't figure out if I'm living G's dream or if my dream is in G's dream and I just can't see it. Do you know what I mean Jesse?"

Jesse wore a puzzled look. Larry continued. "I don't feel like I'm building anything of my own. For the first time in my life I'm not worried about money. I have enough to pay my bills, a beautiful home and car. Nice clothes, I'm around beautiful people so what is wrong with me? Am I living in G's dream that he has built or is my dream in G's dream?"

"Yeah, I get it," said Jesse. "Maybe, G's dream is part of your dream but we make new dreams once we reach the old dream you once had. You just need to step back and think about what or how you want to serve as G always says. I think you have been so busy you have not had a chance to think about a new goal. You have to ask yourself some questions. I am at that same point. I'm asking myself, am I being fulfilled being in Jersey?"

"Could I accomplish more being down here with you guys? You love real estate and you are doing what you love but, you also were a teacher. Maybe you miss the

Challenge of being around high school kids. Maybe you need to build something of your own. Maybe your dream aligned so perfectly with G's dream that you can't see your own," said Jesse.

"Yeah, you're right. Maybe, I can be a part of the camp that G is building down here. I don't need the stress of running it but, I want to be a force in young people's lives. Joy has her properties and Maya has her properties but, I want my own properties on my own land outside of G's."

"I have been thinking about maybe, I could build a daycare center and on the other side of the building be a workspace for entrepreneurs in Jersey City so their children would have a place to learn and play while their parents build their business. I can hire a team to run the daycare center and workspace up there in New Jersey and one down here in North Carolina."

"This way I could feel like I'm building something. You know it's funny how not having enough money to keep a roof over your head and food on the table and paying your other bills. All you can think about is getting money. Then once you have it you start to feel lost and unfulfilled. That's crazy right? Jesse laughs, yeah you never get a chance to see there is more to life than just getting paid but it's hard to see that until all of your needs are met. You truly feel like you are living the life but, when your focus is on making money it's hard to see anything else." "See, this is what I miss," said Larry, "remember our shore vacations and we just dream and talk about how we were going to make it happen? I miss our brother time. I missed you Jesse."

"Yeah I missed you too, Larry. We have to space out sometime on the calendar for the three of us to just talk on a short vacation."

Larry pulled up to his driveway before a Mediterranean house.

"See this is what I'm talking about," said Jesse. "Do you know what my house looks like in Jersey? It's almost 100 years old. It's refurbished on the inside but, man o man, Larry this is living! I really have to reevaluate my own dreams. You know I'm the cautious one out of the three of us and I'm telling you that you have made some good decisions."

"I feel better after talking to you Jesse."

"Yeah, I feel good after talking to you too Larry."

"We still have a lot to accomplish." They went inside to relax and get ready for a surprisingly fun night.

* * *

G.

The phone rang and it was Chip. I was up and refreshed.

"Hello."

"Hey bro, are you ready for tonight?"

"Yeah, did you wrap all of the gifts? I asked.

"Yeah, mom and Bryce and Bella are here with me. They helped me." said Chip.

"Awesome," I replied. "Are you guys coming here or will I meet you?"

"Yeah, it's better if you pick up Joy. I will pick up her mom and Maya and her mom."

"Okay. How many people will be there?"

"All the people who are helping set up for the Winter Fest and some of the store owners on the block. Larry took care of the menu. It's a buffet."

"Ok, I'll call Joy and tell her it's at my hotel at the Harry Belafonte banquet room, right? I said. "Right," said Chip.

I picked up Joy and we pulled up at the hotel. We all met at the Harry Belafonte ballroom.

"Why are we wearing jeans G?"

"Don't worry about it." I chuckled.

"Ok," said Joy, getting out of the car. "If we are the only ones with jeans on then you owe me roses for my office and if everyone has on jeans then I owe you a corn plant for your office."

"Ok, Joy, we're on and I'm letting you know now that I want a tall full corn plant."

Joy laughed, "I'm feeling red, yellow roses G."

They shared a laugh. "Oh well," she said with a sigh to herself. "We'll have a good time anyway." As they went in they started to see people dressed in jeans also.

"Hmm, oh wow, everyone is wearing jeans."

I looked at Joy with a smile. "Tall and full," I said to Joy.

Joy half smiled as she realized she'd just lost the bet. Walking into the ballroom Joy's eyes wandered all over. It was decorated with red and white poinsettia plants. A big Christmas tree with white lights and gifts under the tree. The table had white tablecloths and long wooden runners and on it were mason jars filled with small red and white Christmas balls with white lights.

Mixed in between them were mason jars filled with big red and white gumballs and some jars filled up with round red and white peppermint candy and some mason jars filled with red and white M&M candy and red and white candy kisses mixed throughout.

The place settings were big round red plates, setting mats and on them were white plates and in the middle of the white plate was a red beaded bracelet with a different word on each bracelet. Love, Faith, Hope with a red cloth napkin between each bracelet. Each circular table seats ten people. There were ten tables.

The tables were arranged in U-shapes, the middle of the floor was empty. The room had a Christmas, joyous, fun, happy and earthy feel to it.   I watched Joy's face fill with surprise. She saw Maya and went over to her, drawing me along and said, "Maya this room is beautiful."

Maya was excited to see Joy. "Oh Joy, Larry and Chip did a great job. I'm really impressed. I know that Chip and Larry wanted to put a smile on your face," said Maya.

"They did," said Joy, jumping up and down.

 "Chip and Larry have done a beautiful job," I said.

"I agree G."

"We are going to have a good time tonight," said Joy.

Larry came over with Chip, smiling and feeling good about what they had done to the place. Chip said, "We're all here."

I turned around and glanced at the chip with a smile. I saw them walk over to my mom who found my table.

"Hey mom," he gave her the biggest hug and kiss on the cheek. "Thank you for coming mom. Thank you for flying us down here."

Bryce walked around Starr, their mom, "Hey G, it's looking good here."

"I'm really impressed," she gave him a hug and a kiss. Bella joined and gave a hug. "We all have been talking about moving down here G. when mom retires next year."

"Mom can retire now; you know that right mom?" I said.

"Yes, baby, I know but I only have until July of next year. So, I might as well finish what I started." We laughed. Joy walks over and gives my mom, Starr Graham a hug and a kiss.

"Hello Mrs. Graham. I am so glad you are here." Then she hugged Maya's mom and said hello, "Mrs. Williams, Maya is around here somewhere. Everyone, this is Maya's mom Cherri Williams." "We met already," said Starr, smiling.

Just then Joy mom's came in. She sighted us and joined, "Hello everybody. I'm Rose Oliver, Joy's mom. Chip made sure I got here. I'm so glad to be here. This place is beautiful."

"I'm so glad everyone has on jeans," said Rose.

I looked at Joy who had turned to give her mother a tour of the room. I called, "tall and full, Joy." Joy smiled and said, "you got it G, tall and full."

"Everyone please, come in the party is about to start" the DJ yelled.

I looked around and saw the DJ in the back of the room where Poinsettia was all around the DJ's table. "Oh wow, we got a DJ too."

Joy searched for Maya in excitement. There are too many people in the room now, so she couldn't spot Maya immediately.

Joy and her mom, Maya's mom and my family all sat at the same table. As the music played each table is called out by the DJ to go to the buffet table to get their food.

The different tables were named, Mary, Joseph, Angels, The Stable, frankincense, Gold, Myrrh, Three Wise Men, Camels, Star, Manger.

While the soft Christmas music played in the background people ate and talked. Waiters came to gather the plates at the end. Chip went to the DJ table and took the microphone.

"Hello everyone, my name is Chip for all of you who don't know me. I am G's younger brother. I wanted to wish everyone a Merry Christmas. I know we are all looking forward to this year's WinterFest given by the CEO of the MarketPlace Maya Williams, Joy's best friend."

Everyone clapped.

"For those of you who know Joy, you know she loves playing games. So, we will be playing a game tonight." We cheered.

Larry brought out a chair and set it at the center floor. We had a perfect view.

Chip continued, "there is a number under each seat and that will be called. The person sitting on the chair with that number will come sit in the chair that Larry has just put on the floor. They will be blindfolded and given a wrapped gift. The person will have to guess what is inside of the box by unwrapping the box and feeling it. If they guess correctly, they get to keep the gift if they don't then everyone here gets the gift. Are you ready?"

"Ready!"

Chip grinned and began, "okay, I'm picking table Gold, seat number two. The number is under your chair."

The people at the table Gold were reaching under their seats and someone found the number two.

"I got it," the person shouted.

"Come on up and sit in the chair," Chip invited.

When she got to the seat Larry asked her to give her name then he gave her the microphone.

"Hi everyone. My name is Savannah; my son Cedric has a cupcake business. He has a booth at the festival. Please stop by. Merry Christmas everyone."

"We look forward to seeing you at our booth at the Winter fest."

Chip continued, "now put the blindfold on her Larry."

She put the blindfold on as Larry helped her. Larry gave her a medium size box wrapped in shiny gold paper.

Savannah shook the box. She heard a little rattle then started to open it.

Chip warned, "please do not yell out what it is or no one gets the gift."

Finally, Savannah pulls out clear cellophane wrapping with something wrapped inside. She started to feel but couldn't quite make out what it was.

She said, "a Christmas ornament?"

"No," Chip said. "You can take the blindfold off Savannah."

Anxiously, she took the blindfold off and she saw a note that read, *don't say what is on the square shaped cookies* with a man bent down in front of a woman, a yellow rose in her hair and the name Joy printed under the lady.

Under the man drawn on the cookie the name G. She realized what was inscribed on the cookies and smiles. She said, "they are cookies," and giggled. Then she passed the cookies to Larry.

Larry grinned and said, "you can keep them Savannah and everyone gets cookies."

The waiters came out with a tray of wrapped cookies and started passing them out. Everyone started to cheer. They got a gift. While the gifts were given out, Chip called the next person.

"Joy, since you love games I would like for you to come on up," Joy giggled and glanced at me "Me?" she looked at Chip for confirmation.

"Yes, Joy, come on up." Joy got up and went to the chair. Larry blindfolded her.

She was given a medium sized box wrapped in red sparkly paper. Everyone was ready to see what the gift was and if they would get the gift. As people were receiving their gift they all noticed the picture that was drawn on the cookies. Everyone was surprised. Some people start to gasp.

"Please everyone don't speak, let's give Joy our attention."

I walked over and gave Joy the box. Being blindfolded and not knowing who had given her the box she took it and started to shake it. Everyone laughed and whispered to each other. Joy began to unwrap the box. She pulled out an object with an odd shape.

As she sways her head from side to side, in an effort to figure it out, the room fell quiet.

Then Joy asked, "a small candle?"

Joy began to take the blindfold off; the DJ played the song *You are so beautiful* by Joe Cocker. I serenaded Joy by singing the song. Her surprise was written all over her pretty face. The kids that have a booth at the Winter fest each brought up roses to Joy until she had twelve red and yellow roses.

Listening to the words of the song everyone watched, hypnotized. Joy's brown eyes filled with tears, overcome with happiness. She checked the box in her hand and realized that they were cookies shaped like an engagement ring.

When the record stopped, I got down on one knee, whipped out a box with a real engagement ring in it. I opened the box before her, like the picture on the cookies.

"Joy," I began, "This all started with the sweet gift from Savannah. I called you to help me find a place to live. I bought land and turned it into this wonderful place with you by my side. You make me laugh. You come up with the craziest games for us. You are my voice of reason. You hold my hand when I feel lost. You wink your eye at me when I am on the other side of the room filled with people to let me know I still have your attention. You are an independent woman and boss," my voice cracked as emotions assailed me.

"I want you to be my queen. Ten years from now I want us to tell our children about this moment. Joy, will you marry me?"

Joy palmed my cheeks, blinking away tears, "yes, G. I'll marry you."

I gave a whoop of joy as the entire room erupted with applause and cheer. I placed the ring on her middle finger.

The DJ played Bruno Mars, *Just the way you are.* Chip announced "everyone gets that gift plus the Dreams Come True novel and a blanket to curl up in while you read. Everybody, please get up and celebrate with Parker Graham better known as "G" and Joy Oliver on the dance floor." While people got on the dance floor to dance with us, the waiters gave out cookies shaped like an engagement ring, cupcakes that read, "she said, Yes" on them, and the beautifully wrapped book and blanket.

At the table Maya and her mom Cherri and Joy's mom Rose and G's mom Starr and her daughters Bryce and Bella were brimming with happiness for us.

"The fellas really pulled this off nicely," said Maya.

"They sure did," said Starr.

Bryce and Bella got up to dance. Larry came to Maya and asked with a puppy-dog expression, "Maya, please dance with me?"

Maya said, "you guys did a great job in keeping it a secret."

"Don't be mad," Larry begged. "We just wanted you and Joy to know we got you. You don't always have to be in charge. Relax, and let us work. Let us be King up in here."

She laughed, "Okay, you got that. I like knowing you guys can take charge."

She got up and followed Larry to the dance floor. Starr, Rose and Cherri conversed, occasionally bursting into laughter. They got to know each other, while enjoying the music until three older men asked each of the ladies to dance with them.

Starr gave the handsome slightly gray headed man a quick once-over and said, "why, thank you" as they strutted off to the dance floor. Another with a bald head, well-shaven and stout, came up to Rose and asked her to dance. She accepted demurely.

A tall man with a bald head, and a gray beard, waited for the other men to leave, then said to Cherri, "hello beautiful, may I have the pleasure of dancing with you?" he held out a hand. Cherri accepted the proffered hand and headed to the floor. They celebrated the engagement far into the night.

Black America Village

A few days later, G waited for Danny as he got off the train.

"Hey, Danny, thanks for coming," said G. "How was your trip?"

"It was pretty nice," Danny replied. They began to walk toward G's car. "I got a chance to relax and listen to a guy by the name, Calvin Michaels. he's a Youtuber."

"Oh, I've heard of him," G said. "I love listening to good conversation and hearing other people's perspectives on current events."

Danny was amazed that G listened to the same YouTuber.

"Have you ever heard of David Shands?" asked G. "He's a YouTuber. His show is called *Social Proof*. He's a friend in my head."

Danny replied, "no I've never heard of him."

"Well, I have a few people along with me that have paid to join his show. The *Morning meet up.com* is the best investment to building success that I know of right now. On Monday through Friday from eight A.M. to Nine A.M. all entrepreneurs get on a Zoom call and we share and grow from all kinds of people killing it in the game."

"You can't help but walk away inspired and ready to go. I want all of my team to join. So, get ready. The secret sauce to David Shands is, he's a black man keeping the black community awake by interviewing rich black people. I have to talk to Maya and see if she can get him to come out here and talk to her kids in her entrepreneur program."

Danny said to G, "I knew I liked you. You know good people when you listen to them."

G chuckled, assuming Danny referred to how they met. "Here we are. I'll open the trunk so you can put your suitcase in."

"Thanks G."

While they boarded the car, G said, "we are on our way to the camp. I want you to see it before it gets dark. Then I have dinner set up for us and a couple of friends and my brother back at my house. We can talk more about the things we are doing and how you can be a part of it."

Danny was elated. It was great to be a part of something that he really wanted to do.

Riding in the car with G, Danny's eyes were everywhere, checking out the scenery. He saw a cotton field that was once filled with cotton as far as the eyes can see. He'd never been to this part of North Carolina before. Danny was enjoying the ride. He saw piles of hay, some had Santa Clause faces drawn on them. Some had three rows of hay stacked on top of each other decorated like a snowman with the hat and the red scarf. One had a reindeer's face with cutout antlers. Some had red bows wrapped around them, they resembled Christmas presents.

Lola would love it here, Danny thought as he watched the unfolding Christmas scenery. Kids laughing while riding on a hayride looking at the Christmas light show. Then we passed Santa in a sleigh with presents and parents and their kids took turns waiting to take pictures with Santa. A little bit further down the road is a farmer's market store with all kinds of goodies. Not long after riding we turned into the entrance of a gated Community that had two large water fountains on each side of the gate that displayed a colorful water show. In the middle of each fountain there was a 12 ft. vigorously robust bronze statue of each guardian angel that was kneeled down on one knee looking up to the heavens with a large sword in his hand facing down. Each angle had huge white feathered wings with gold tips. Each angel was bald headed and very handsome. This place is beautiful.

G turned into the gateway to the community. On the drive, we passed by a big parking lot on the right and left side. There were grayish-blue trolley car buses that had a big flag of a mural of Harriet Tubman holding her hand out to bring you to freedom in 3d. I have never seen anything like it. Black America Village was the name of the trolley car and Freedom was the name of another trolley car. There were visitors from all over the United States. Danny could see from their license plates as they rode by. People parked their cars to board the buses to take a tour of Black America village.

"They drive to the community and pay a fee to get on the buses," said G. "They tour the area and stop for lunch and shopping at the end."

G continued straight ahead until Danny could hear music. The sound was all over the air.

"Is that Erica Campbell and Lashawn Daniels singing *I Luh God, You don't luh God what's wrong with you?*" Danny asked, bobbing his head. The beat of the music touched the soul as the sound got louder. He began to feel like getting out of the car to dance and praise God. Danny couldn't help it. He had to ask.

"G, this music we are listening to, where is it coming from?"

G smiled, happy that Danny noticed. He wanted to see Danny's reaction to Black America village. "Oh, says G there are speakers hidden around the trees under fake rocks and yes, that is them singing and rapping. There is soul in the old and new gospel music. There are other

170

artists that you may hear also like Tye Tribbett, singing *We gonna be alright,* or Kirk Franklin You can't help but be filled with the Holy Spirit when you come here. This is the black culture experience."

G continued driving down a long road until they came to a two-lane security gate going in and two lanes out. On the top of the tall security building was a larger than life like huge 3D black screen that read in white lights, *Welcome to Black America village.*

Then it played a short video of black kids dancing and praising God in the streets.

"This is incredible!" Danny gazed at the sign and rubbed his eyes to make sure that he was reading it right.

G looked at Danny and asked, "are you okay?"

Danny replied, "oh, yes I'm okay." Danny glanced around, "Is this gated community named Black America Village?"

"Yes, said G as the system read his license plate. The gates lifted so he could drive through. In the other lane cars were stopped by security before they could enter. Danny was beyond stunned and anxious to see more. He gazed at him, as they drove further, they came upon a huge roundabout that had a sign that read in separate bold letters, Welcome to Black America Village with flags showing a vibrant picture of Harriet Tubman holding her hand out to take you to freedom in 3D. The same design was on the trolley cars. Danny could see in the short distance a twelve feet tall bronze statue of a woman holding a lantern. There were five other statues beside it.

Two women and three men. Danny's mouth dropped open.

"That's a statue of Harriet Tubman holding a lantern with slaves behind her, bringing them to freedom. At night the lantern lights up," G explained.

"That's awesome! I have never seen anything like it."

The statues were in the middle of a wide divider that separated the cars driving into the community and the cars driven out of the community. There was another big sign in the lights overhead that read *Welcome to Black America Village.*

As far as Danny could see there were wide dividers down the middle of the wide streets. On each divider there were colorful magical water features that sprouted up out of the pavers. Carved out at the end of each divider was a walkway for people to wait until the light turned green.

Each crosswalk was painted over the pavers with colorful artwork that led the pedestrians across the street to get to the other sidewalk. The place was vibrant, festive, filled with positive energy and soul. The street signs read in a purple background with yellow letters: *Black Wall Street* and the cross street read *Harriet Tubman Way*.

When G drove past the stores that lined the streets, Danny noticed murals on one of the sides of the building by the street corner. 3D pictures of the Cotton Club, The Apollo and the Savoy with black people dressed up, on their way in. "Wow, who is the artist that did all of the murals and the flag?" Danny, beaming.

"Oh, my sister Bella is an artist and she knows the artist Michael Rosato who is an extraordinary artist located in Cambridge Maryland. He did the mural for the Harriet Tubman museum and educational center. She was mesmerized by Michael Rosato's paintings. After agreeing to his fees he did the murals for Black America Village."

They continued onto the red, orange, yellow, blue, and white, brick row houses with storefronts on the ground level. He could see a coffee shop with tables and chairs that were in front of the brick face row house and behind the table and chairs was a glass door and glass windows. With a sign on the glass window saying *Black America Village coffee café*. People walked by and a couple sat at the table with heated lamps.

"Wow, It's chilly out but, people will come out anyway," Danny mused.

The sidewalks and streets were made of blue and gray brick pavers. The brick row houses with stores and restaurants on the ground level felt festive. Some had black shutters that made the windows pop. Some had window boxes, pine branches and Christmas garlands with lights and ornaments in the boxes draped down giving the brick row house character with a matching color black door. Some had steps with black iron railings that lead to the first floor. Potted plants graced the sides of the doorway. The sidewalks made of blue and gray brick pavers were wide enough for tables and chairs that had hanging lights of stars and Christmas ornaments of different colors and sizes hung over the tables that had enough room for people to walk by without being in the way of those dining out. The street has trees that are lit up at night with white lights, giving a soothing atmosphere.

Each street divider held a statue of a black person that had shaped the black community.

"Is that a statue of Martin Luther King and his wife Corretta Scott king holding hands and waving at cars go by?" Danny questioned in disbelief.

"Yes," G chuckled.

"This place is amazing."

On the side streets Danny spots more lifelike 3D graffiti paintings on buildings. One was of children playing stickball in the streets and on the other side girls played jump rope. Another group of kids played hula hoops in the street. Further down, a wall museum with Jet and Ebony magazine, Count Basie, Billie Holiday, Ella Fitzgerald, Nancy Wilson, Aretha Franklin, Sammy Davis Jr., Duke Ellington, Quincy Jones, Michael Jackson, Prince 2Pac, Biggie and other famous people.

They drove by an art gallery, a quilt shop, a T-shirt and hoodie shop, a toy store, a waffle shop, a café, a bookstore, an ice cream shop, a candy store filled with all kinds of candy in barrels, a general store, a private movie theater, a museum of black history, an arts and craft store, a few American food restaurants, a couple of tourist shops, a couple of boutiques, a couple of shoe stores, a place called *Little People Fun Place.* It had blow up houses, mazes, arcade games and toys for the kids to play with, party rooms for birthdays, a camera shop, a small music studio for anyone who wanted to have fun and sing, painting party shop with rooms for drinking wine and having desserts while painting for different party groups, bakery, couple of soul food restaurants and barbecue restaurant. People were out and about going in and out of stores.

"I love this place!" Danny screamed.

They were at the end of *Black Wall Street*. There was another roundabout with a little island. On it is a huge billboard similar to the one atop the security building. This one had in season flowers and grass with Poinsettias at the base of the billboard. The billboard advertised the stores on Black *Wall Street* and all of the events happening that month. *The Winter Blessing festival* was happening in a few days.

As G drove by the roundabout, the road continued and led to the end of the street.

"This street is called G Way."

Danny thought, *wow, that name's interesting.* There was a huge strip mall with only three buildings and about hundred and fifty parking spaces that separated the lake from the street. The strip had an elegant hotel. The front of the hotel faced Black Wall Street and on the other side of the hotel faced the lake. The hotel had twelve floors. It had a soft white color with large glass windows everywhere. There was an atrium on the inside of the hotel. A few hundred feet away from the hotel was a single floor flea market warehouse of a food market.

Baked foods, cooked foods, fresh fruits, vegetables and beverages. There was also a stage on the wide pier that extended out to a deck over the lake where Community entertainers sang, danced and played music in the summer. G explained to Danny. "Oh and I forgot to tell you that, the hotel has a glass enclosed pier that leads to a glass enclosed gazebo filled with green plants and beautiful flowers spread over the deck that sits over the lake where people can sit and eat from the restaurant, an extension from the hotel. About a few hundred feet on the other side of the hotel is a warehouse building of vendors who sell arts and crafts, antiques and the building also has a pier that leads to a deck. That one has a merry go round and a train for kids and adults to ride."

"The children and the parents love the train ride and play area."

Danny nodded and stared down the street on G way. He noticed a gated area with security where cars drove in and out. Then he checked the other side on G way and noticed another gated area with security. He was in awe and wondered where those two gated communities led to. Then G interrupted his thoughts.

"This gated area to our left is where the camp is located. To our right, on G way is the gated housing area."

"Wow, it just keeps going and getting better and better," Danny said.

G pulled up to the hotel, "this is where you will be staying."

"Wow, this place just doesn't seem real." Danny said in wonder.

"What makes you say that?" asked G.

"Well, I'm wondering if Black America Village is a community that is black targeted or black owned?"

"Huh?" G asked again.

"What I mean is, this place is filled with black culture. It feels so good to be here. I was just wondering if someone white developed it for black people?"

G just stared ahead at Black Wall Street. "Wow, you think white people would develop a place like this for black people?" His voice was laced with mild amusement.

"Well, white people buy black businesses and get black people to continue to think they are supporting a black business when really it is a white business now."

G smiled, "well this, Danny, is black owned."

"How I wish that was true," Danny said with disappointment.

"It's true Danny because I developed Black America Village," said G.

Danny was stunned. He tried to hide the shock and embarrassment as he alighted. G did the same, looking mystified.

"What's wrong Danny?"

He looked around with his mouth wide open and his arms spread open as though he was trying to embrace the Village. He said in a low tone, "you developed this place?"

"Yes," G chuckled.

"For somebody white who owns this village?" he squinted his eyes, waiting for G, to confirm that someone white owns the place.

"Noooooo," G, drawled. "I used my own money." G looked at him seriously.

He was amazed and shocked. "All of this is you?"

"Yeah," G said, sounding more relaxed. As he leaned against G's SUV he marveled at it all. Then it suddenly occurred to him.

"Wow, so you're rich? I mean you have to be in order to do all of this. Who are you? How did I get on your radar?"

"I'm not rich. I'm just a hopeless veteran who is trying to figure out my life now that I am out of the military. It's hard to survive out here on these streets. I'm not fancy G. I'm just a regular guy." He couldn't help the embarrassment surging through him about his position in life. G walked over to him, and leaned on the car beside him and said, "I'm just a regular guy just like you Danny. I'm a black man that was a teacher in a black inner city. I worked with a lot of white teachers and a white principal. It was hard. I felt like I was in a fight every day. Students not wanting to attend class, or able to read their books or solve math equations. I tried to keep the students engaged while dealing with single parents who would get off from work and be too tired to even look to see if their children have done their homework.

"Not to mention white teachers not understanding black people's culture or struggle. Their way of teaching does not resonate with black students. White people's points of reference were different. It's hard for each group to relate to each other. Living in a building in the inner city is different from living in a house in the suburbs. What I see outside of my door is different from what white people see outside of their door. Wearing this color skin with this kind of hair is different from white people."

"Our black kids feel the difference every day. Looking at someone who looks like them and who shares the same struggle gets their attention. That was me, I was that teacher. I didn't want to lose my students to the streets."

"The same streets that I grew up in. I started to feel trapped, limited. I felt like I had stopped growing. I started feeling like I wanted more out of life but I didn't know what that was. The last day of school I had a student by the name of Cedric. His mom's name was Savannah. She sent him to school with a card for me. It was a beautiful card thanking me for helping her son get through a tough year for him."

"She is a single parent getting home from work not being on top of making sure he understood his lessons and doing his homework. I filled in that gap like I tried to do with all of my students. When the last day of class was over and the students had gone, I sat back down at my desk thinking about going to the Jersey Shore on my summer vacation and I looked down and saw the card and decided to open it. To my surprise, there was a hundred-dollar bill inside the card."

"It was too late to give the money back, the kids were gone. So I decided to get some magazines to read while I was on the beach. I went to a news stand and saw people online to get lottery tickets and scratch offs. Then that small window of opportunity opened. I struggled for a while, to buy or not to buy a ticket, then I went for it."

"A white guy jumped in front of me and grabbed the tickets I was going to buy. Frustrated and dealing with the disrespect, I managed to hold it together. To only decide on buying some other scratch offs. Then I asked for four tickets, hung up on another display. When I found out how much they cost. I was too embarrassed to leave them there so I brought them. I walked out pissed and feeling taken advantage of."

"I didn't know it at the time but I brought a winning scratch off worth a hundred million dollars. Danny turned to G and grinned. For once the black man won!

"White privilege worked in our favor that time." They both laugh.

"Yeah, you're right," said G.

"Wow, I'm really happy for you but out of all of the things you could have done with your money why this?" Danny asked.

"I didn't start out with this place in mind. I just wanted a change. I wanted to buy some land and build a house on it while I figured out what I was going to do next. Then I met my fiancée Joy and her best friend Maya. Joy is so grounded. She's like a foundation that motivates me to keep growing. She has her own real estate company. That's how we met. She was my realtor. Her friend Maya is an advocate for the youth. She started a fair that helps kids who wanted to be entrepreneurs. She teaches them about business and helps them create a business so they can sell whatever it is that they have to sell. The fair she started was very successful. There were only black vendors. So, that got me thinking about what if I created a black wall street where we could have black owned businesses. Having Maya's fair here we had created a black wall street not even realizing it until the fair came together."

"So, I got my brother who has his own construction business. Helped me put this project together. He knew how to build a team and subcontracted work out and he has not stopped since."

Danny interjected, "but how do I fit into this larger-than-life dream of yours?"

"Let's get you checked into the hotel. You still have more to see."

After Danny got checked in G took him to another connected gated community where the camp was situated. After G's license plate was read at security, he drove around on the other side of the lake.

"What are you going to name this camp?"

"The Black America Village Camp."

"I like that. Why did you name this gated community Black America Village?"

"I wanted a place for descendants of slaves who built this country to have a place that belonged to them. Like, Little Italy or China town. I wanted to create an environment of hope. I wanted to create an environment where black boys don't have to walk in fear of policemen jumping to conclusions and killing them. So, I hired security instead."

"This camp is for kids to be kids and build their character and self-esteem. To get away from the insanity of living in the inner city for a while."

"Yeah, G, living in the projects is almost the same as living in a combat outpost in Afghanistan. I lived in fear every day. I tried not to think about it. Being out there with my unit gave me some sense of safety. We had to look out for each other if we all wanted to come back home alive."

Danny bobbed his head, "I understand that these kids may feel the same way. That's why they are in gangs in order to belong in a unit. Their enemy is not with each other when you think about it. A lot of kids have similar home issues. All sides are in the same financial dilemma. We grow up believing the narrative that selling drugs, playing sports or entertainment is the only way out."

"If the government wants to get rid of people all they have to do is put them in an environment where there is little to no resources and soon they will attack each other. Then you don't have to get rid of them. They will get rid of each other."

Danny grimaced and continued, "we want to get around the rich elite people in control of our poor environment that we live in so badly to show we made it out. Not realizing that they are the enemy that has us destroying each other. They pay us little to nothing in wages and then take almost half of that away in taxes. Then what's left to pay rent and we barely have enough to eat and buy clothes. This camp has to be for building wisdom and knowledge and learning a skill."

"G, when you have a skill you are your own boss. You set the price. I'll look into veterans who have skills and who'd want to teach the kids. I'll also put a team together and reach out to trade schools that will give a discount for kids who want to continue learning about a trade. Then I can work on starting a website for the kids to zoom in and learn a trade from the teachers we hire to earn extra income. We all win. I know Malik, the owner from the barber shop that I work with, would love to teach. I know my brother-in-law won't mind teaching a trade in contracting work."

"They can teach the course on the website we pay someone to develop and the kids' parents can pay for the kids to take the course. G, the kids have to go back with hope and knowledge with a dream that they didn't come here with. This place is peaceful. I can see the kids learning critical thinking from a veteran. I can see the kids sitting in areas all around the campgrounds writing down their thoughts."

"I can see them making new friends. I can see them learning about eating healthy food. I will get a holistic doctor that can teach the kids about minerals and green vegetables so they can learn how to be healthy. I can see the kids on teams playing games and overcoming obstacle courses."

"I can see the kids paddle boating and swimming at the lake. I can see the kids zip lining from one fort to another. I can see the kids and lots and lots of tables eating in the cabin hall. Where we will also have a dance on their last night being here."

"I see the kids in small cabins that sleep six to eight kids with four bathrooms. There will be a terrace connected to each cabin for them to sit on at their break time and share their experiences being here at the camp. Each cabin is painted in soothing colors and the Black America Village flag hangs beside it. One cabin will be painted

Sky-blue, and one light brown, and one sage green. I think that we should build this camp for fun and give hope as our mission."

G was hypnotized by Danny's visions. "I knew when I read your goals on your *Go Fund Me* page it was going to be a good fit for this camp. Danny, I love your visions. You have a lot of work ahead of you. So you have to start building a team right away if we are going to be open by the summer."

"Thank you, I can't wait."

"I will introduce you to my brother and the architect. You can tell them the visions you have and they can incorporate them with the buildings and cabins that are already built. The rest of the year the camp will be used for different companies or organizations that want to rent the spaces out for conferences, or seminars. Even weddings or parties are welcome to rent."

"I can't help but be in awe of you G. You are reaching back pulling your people up with you. When you could be looking down on them. Watching them look up at you wishing they could be like you."

G beamed at the compliment, then he said, "Danny, I want you to speak to a lawyer after you write out your business plan for all of your ideas. Then package your curriculum to sell online to people who are interested in the vision."

Out of the gated camp on the opposite side of the community, there was another security gate with guards that directed people to houses.

"Who lives over there G?"

"I do, along with other black people. I have built two-, three- and four-bedroom houses there. There are seventy-five rental houses here and five B&B's. We have by-laws that we all abide by. I'm trying to create a peaceful environment for the residents."

"Okay, Danny, now that our tour's complete. I have some other meetings I have to attend. I'll drop you at the hotel. I'll be back to get you for dinner at my house where you will meet my friends and my brother."

"Ok, G, I'm going to lay down and rest for a while. I'm feeling a little bit overwhelmed with happiness."

"Then I'm doing a good job Danny. I will call you in a couple of hours before I come and get you."

"Alright, looking forward to meeting your family."

Danny alighted and entered the hotel.

Brotherhood Bonding

A couple of hours had gone by, Danny was in the car with G surveying the gated community adjacent Black Wall Street.

"How was your hotel room, Danny?"

"It was beautiful. Toward the elevator there was a 3D waterfall that went across the entire wall starting from the top. So, when I walked into the elevator it felt like I was going to get wet walking into the waterfall. It was jaw dropping, as in amazing!"

"You own the hotel too, G?"

"Yes, I have to have a place for guests that come to visit Black America Village to stay. By the way my sister Bella and another artist she picked did the artwork on the walls."

Danny shook his head in disbelief, it was overwhelming for him to take in.

Gazing out the car window, Danny was amazed at the beautiful earth tones, browns, blues, greens, tans, and grays, stucco and concrete houses and other styled houses with respective lawns and backyards. Even there, Christmas decorations glinted off the walls. The community had a different look and feel than the Black Wall Street hustle and bustle feel. It was calmer and peaceful. It almost felt like an upper-class community.

Cul-de-sacs and winding streets with sidewalks and streets made of blues and grays brick pavers. Now, they drove past a thriving park. There were swings and sliding boards.

"I was just wondering..." Danny began.

"Yeah?"

"Do black people live here?"

"Yes," he replied with a chuckle. "exclusively."

Excitement strummed Danny's nerves. The shimmering lake glinted between the cul-de-sacs.

Without warning G swung into a paved circular driveway, before a large craftsman style house and a three-car garage that was connected next to the house. There was a fountain at the center of the paved driveway. The fountain was surrounded by big, round gray and tan stones. The insides were decorated with a water feature that lit up in different colors at night. The color of G's house was blue with six white trim gables that featured brackets.

It had a stained wood pergola that covered the front door and extended out to the circular driveway. A few cars were already parked in the driveway.

"This is it. Welcome to my home."

"It's beautiful."

Danny hadn't digested Black America Village. Now, he wondered how G was so down to earth? He seemed relatable until a person saw that he created a community and literally had a home on the lake. The front door was huge, constructed with stained wood. There was a huge, glassed opening above the door that was built to light the foyer. Danny trailed G as they stepped into the large well-lit vaulted ceilinged foyer.

G called to the laughing group, "hello everybody. My new friend, Danny, is here."

"Hello Danny!" was chorused at me.

Smiling, Danny said, "hello,"

He noticed that the room had creamy white walls with stained wood trims and vaulted ceilings. It was an open floor plan. A large fluffy bluish-gray couch dominated the center. Wide pillory blue chairs with wide ottomans that faced the chairs.

Danny turned in a circle, then he looked at the fellas seated around a large waterfall island that separated the kitchen from the living room.

"I'm sorry I just can't stop looking around. My name is Danny."

"I'm Chip, G's younger brother."

"I'm Larry, G's best friend. I live down the road."

"I'm Jesse, G's other best friend and I live in New Jersey. Please take a seat and have dinner with us."

"Thank you," Danny said. He walked toward an unoccupied stool by the kitchen Island. He noticed the stairs by the side of the room, leading up to the catwalk that overlooked the living room and kitchen. G nodded at Danny to dish his food as others had done.

"So, Jesse," G started, "how is life in New Jersey? Are you ready to move down here yet?"

"Things are okay at home but, honestly I miss you guys. Now you've developed this place, it's very appealing. I've been wondering if I could live and make a living here. I mean it's embarrassing to admit but I'm kind of feeling stuck and unappreciated at the school in New Jersey. I feel the principal's methods won't allow the kids to grow. Culture's unsuitable and different."

"How so?" G asked.

"As one of the guidance counselors, we should have a bigger presence in the high school. The technology that we have today, we didn't have twenty years ago. Jobs are being eliminated because of new technology. I remember when students went to college and got into debt to become journalists. Now, just start your own YouTube channel. Some of these YouTubers are making more money than the journalist with the debt and degree."

"So I ask myself, what should the students learn? What should their goals be? Is college the only answer? This principal has an old way of looking at things. The faculty needs a new approach to keep our students engaged."

"Our students are going home where their parents are struggling to make ends meet. Is this the destination from going to school? Struggle?" This is what the kids are thinking."

"In the inner city they are forced to grow up fast to survive. We have to meet them where they are. We need to expose them to different trades so they can acquire new skills. There is more to life than selling drugs, stealing cars, gambling, scamming. But those are the only opportunities that present themselves in the inner cities. It is our job to show them more productive opportunities so they don't end up with a dead-end job or worse, jail.

"I agree. These outdated methods should be stricken. What do you suggest?" G asked.

"G, we need field trips to businesses. Our students should be taken out of the Community to see a place like this. They can see what's possible. Our students need to hear from business owners who didn't go to college but they are making a good living for themselves. Like contractors, steel workers, carpenters, plumbers, electricians, trucking, ceramists, seamstresses, mechanics just to name a few. The old way of just preparing for college should be abolished. Do you know how our kids are learning how to deal with stress, G?"

"Stress at home because there may not be enough food or a parent may be on drugs or locked up. Oh, or the boyfriend is beating up their mom. They learn not to speak out because this is normal for them. Then when they get older, they are taught to do what they gotta do to get money and use a gun to defend themselves and their family or gang members."

"They join gangs because there is no advocate for them at home. It's a vicious cycle and it takes a village to break it. Who knows maybe Black America Village could be the catalyst to start to make things change?"

"Some of these kids spend more time in school than they do at home with their parents. That's why, I'm starting to feel like I'm not being a team player because these guidelines on teacher's morale and student's morale are not effective."

"I'm starting to feel like my self-esteem is being chipped away. It's starting to affect my health. I'm taking high blood pressure pills now. This is crazy. In The Evening, I come home to finish the bottle of whisky I got two days ago because I feel powerless. This subliminal feeling of white privilege blurs the line. Somehow, I wonder if the blows for a black man are less forceful when he is financially independent."

"When he can up and relocate if his environment is not conducive to his standards. You work hard, and what do you have to show for it? More struggle? Then I come down here and it looks like everyone is thriving. I feel like I am missing out. I can feel the impact that you have on the people that come from all over the United States to see Black America Village. The camp, businesses, not to mention the houses that you have built and rented out in the community. This place is a go to destination."

"The struggle is real G, anybody would have taken their winnings and never looked back. How you mentally discipline yourself to serve others, I'll never understand."

G interrupted Jesse, "let me tell you why I wanted to be a teacher. When I was younger I had a hard time in class, I always wished I had a teacher who could give me a better understanding of the subjects that I was trying to understand. I always failed classes. I almost gave up, to be honest. My mother pitched when she could but four kids and two jobs didn't let her do much."

"One day, I saw the movie, *To Sir with Love* starring Sidney Poitier. A black man that made me realize how powerful I could be too. He was a teacher who understood the kid's weaknesses and got the importance of dealing with the whole person and not just the education. He went deeper than the school's curriculum. He saw lost kids and that needed guidance, which he gave them with love. He gave them permission to fail and to keep trying, they did. They all graduated. Then I knew I wanted to be that man *Sidney Poitier.* I decided to be a teacher."

"Though he wanted to be an engineer and make more money. He saw how badly he was needed. He could make a difference. He threw out the lesson plan and met the kids at their specific points of need. He taught them hygiene, to respect themselves and each other. He taught them his way and the kids loved him for it.

"That movie has kept me grounded. I believe you have to see who you want to become to stay on course. Sidney Poitier was that man for me."

Danny listened to Jesse and G, he realized that he wasn't the only one who was trying to find their way. He was amazed by the entire program. The place gave the feeling of hope that was desperately needed within the black community.

"I remember," said Jesse, "when we were on vacation and we talked about what you were going to do now that you'd won the lottery."

"You thought hard about it. You were not sure but you knew you wanted to make a difference in people's lives and you have done that. I am so proud to be your friend. I never realized how unselfish you were. Looking at what you've built for people of color to share and build a life in, is remarkable."

"Larry and Chip had been with you every step of the way."

"Yes," G agreed with a proud smile at his brother and friend. "But, I could not have done any of this without the guidance of God."

"This vision developed over time, Jesse. I didn't see this when we were younger and frolicking at the beach."

"Savannah, a single mother, gave me a token of her appreciation. I went the extra mile to get help for her son Cedric with his schoolwork. I was motivated to do so because I have seen what a lack of guidance and hope can do to a child. That could have been me if it wasn't for my mother. She couldn't help me with all of my schoolwork but she made sure we were productive in the church club, the community center, or chores around the house."

"Joy and Maya came later. Those two women have made a major impact on me and my direction. I believe that God put them in my path to lead me in this direction. Again, I am very grateful to God and my close circle of family and friends."

"We miss you too Jesse but we know that everyone has to follow their own path. You are always welcome down here though."

"That's why Danny is here. I want him to be part of the camp program and if he likes to stay on I would love for him to be part of the community center.

"I listened to a black billionaire, uh... Robert F. Smith. He talked about his dream to get little black kids to take coding like they did sports. I'll have coding included at the community center and teach kids trades in the building. Not everyone wants to go to college like you said. We could use you at the camp Jesse. You could make sure that the kids from Jersey City could come down here for summer camp. You could build a network of schools from there to come down here."

"I have Mike, my accountant and a couple of Financial advisors and their teams that had helped me structure a Non-profit Organization for Black America Village for the programs covering each student to come here for a week or two. It will include transportation."

"I have more than one team for my finances. I don't give one team all of my money to manage because my mother always told me, *you don't put all of your eggs in one basket because you just might lose it.*

"The foundation that I have now will donate money towards the expenses. We have black sponsors. I know that some working parents just don't have the money for camp programs and our kids need to get away to replenish themselves."

"You could get the kids so they'd learn about themselves and grow in a positive direction. Maybe that's a business that you and Larry can start and work with me as an independent contractor."

"A scared man never gets nowhere!" exclaimed Larry. Maybe this is the answer that I was looking for. Something that we can do outside of G's shadow."

"Think about it man." Larry continued. G has treated us with respect and has looked out for all of us. I have a house. Chip has one too. His mom and sisters, the same. The only stipulation is that if we decide to sell the house, G gets the first option to buy the house back."

"To be honest with you G, I wanted to talk to you about relocating down here after the school year is over," said Jesse.

"It's done as far as I'm concerned Jesse," said G. I have 2 empty houses on the block that Larry lives in, It's for air B&B's. We can look at them tomorrow, make your choice and I'll stop renting out when you're ready to move in. My interior decorator can tune it up to your style."

Everyone stared at Jesse, to hear what he had to say.

Jesse teared up, "I feel so unworthy. I stayed in New Jersey because I honestly felt that in spite of the white privilege that I experienced I could still make a difference with the students and faculty. I wanted to prove you guys wrong for leaving New Jersey. But maybe you're right G, maybe I can still help them just another way. I'm not leaving them altogether."

G scraped his chair back and went to hug Jesse. "We know you. We know you are the cautious one of the group. You keep us balanced, man. You analyze everything and that's important. To have someone around to help us to see something we might have missed. We love you unconditionally. We just love you for who you are and have been," G said.

"Yeah, we'll even get you a girlfriend when you get down here," said Larry. They all laughed.

"I know you're not talking Larry. What's going on with you and that bossy woman you need a vacation from in New Jersey?" Jesse joked.

"Okay," G broke in before the banter really got started.

"We're back to normal like old times."

"Yeah," said Larry with a smile.

"After she told me it was time for me to come back, I had to let her go," Larry answered Jesse's question about his woman.

As Danny listened, he became more inquisitive about G's lifestyle and how he brought many opportunities to black people. It was his chance to join the conversation.

"Ah, I have a question G, If you don't mind my asking."

"Not at all, Danny. What's up?"

Their curious faces made him nervous but he forged on. "I have been in a brain freeze ever since I found out you were super rich today. It's a lot to process. I'm just trying to catch up with this mindset. We are in this banging house and no one but me is freaked out about it!" Danny shook his head in astonishment.

"Oh," laughed Chip, "we've done that already."

"Yeah," said Larry, "it took all of us time to wrap our brains around G's winnings. We gave him some space to think about what he was going to do with his money but, meanwhile we were excited so you would've thought it was our personal win."

"Oh, and I remember when me, the builders and the rest of the team completed building this house for G. Larry and I spent the night with G, so we could experience the place firsthand."

"The only one here that's rich is G," said Chip.

"What makes this a beautiful experience is having family and friends that enjoy everything with me. I continue to pray for guidance every step of the way not to let my ego become bigger."

Danny smiled and gathered the courage to ask a burning question. "Ah, G?"

"Yeah?"

"We had Tulsa where black people were thriving, white people burned it down."

"Are you concerned that it could happen again? It's because of Greenwood that I thought this was even possible. Black people are resilient. We survived slave ships and now we go on cruises. We were slaves in the fields that we didn't own, now a lot of us own those very fields. We learned to read in secret now we're taught in schools. We have to sit on the back of buses now, some of us own buses."

"When the World Trade Center was razed, the first thing the elite rich white men said was, let's rebuild. Black people face fear, live in fear and triumph in spite of fear. We have to keep rebuilding! As our people sang during the civil rights movement, "*We shall overcome some day!*"

"We have to keep rebuilding, our ancestors that've been hung, raped, shot and overdosed from drugs placed in our communities so we could destroy each other. Would have said, Rebuild! Keep going like they kept going!"

Danny was proud of G, just by listening to his speech, everyone reflected his feelings in their nods.

"Can I ask you another question G?"

"Sure, anything. You don't have to keep taking permission."

"Thank you, uh... do you still experience racism being rich?"

"Oh, we have had this conversation before," Larry chimed in as Larry and Chip laughed.

"That's a good question Danny, and the answer is yes. Nobody really knows me. I'm not famous and I don't carry myself like I am rich. I don't have a flashy car. I dress comfortably. My house is really nice but it doesn't stand out from the other houses on the block. When I go out to a very nice restaurant no one gives me any special attention. I can feel the way I'm treated and see the condescending looks that I get sometimes."

"White businessmen have that air of priority when you're in their presence. It stinks and I don't frequent those places. I think what helps me deal with it a lot better than I used to, is because I know I don't need these people for anything. My family and I are going to be alright. I have more choices than I did before. I can walk in my truth with a lot less fear now. I can say what I mean without worrying if I'll be out of a job by the next day.

"I noticed that white privilege is on every financial level that black people live on. The black people that are on the same financial level as rich white people, the rich white people will never let the rich black people in their close-knit circle."

"If it looks like black people are in their circle, it's just an illusion to make working black think they're in. I don't care how much money you have. You can be worth a billion dollars and white people will always see your color and find a way to use your color and your platform to make more billions off of you but, without including you."

"Black people think their money has earned them the right to sit at their table and to be respected but the subtle disparaging messages are still eminent."

"You will never hear rich black people complain to the poor or working black people about how they are being discriminated against with rich white people, because that would destroy the facade that some rich black people have created for us to think that they are better than the rest of the poor and working black people.

"Oh," said Chip, "and white people want to extend the facade by dangling the rich carrot in front of us to make black people think that getting rich is obtainable for us all when they know that white people have not made this a fair playing field."

"Now, let the rich black people keep buying all of the rich white people's jewelry, clothes, sneakers, and cars and liquor. Give the white men your money you earned, make them even richer but black people will never be one of the good old boys. No matter how hard they try."

"I have heard some white businessmen ask black people to be partners in their companies. Then they apply for grants and loans that are put in place for black and minority people only."

"When the white man's company gets the money they kick the black man to the curb and there is nothing we can do about it. Some black people believe the lie and fall for the scam then they realize they'd been used."

"This is not a fair playing field for black people," said Larry.

"That's why it is so important to build your own table. Like Tyler Perry and Master P have done," said G. "Pull another black person up when you get to the next level. You never know, one day you may need that person you helped."

"If we don't create our own and stop trying to sit at someone else's table we will always be used and disrespected."

G continued, "That's why I built this place. We can do this. If we did it before in Oklahoma, Florida and New York and other places. We can do it again."

Larry chimed in, "have you ever bought something and thought you were supporting a black business to only find out it was a white business after all?"

"Look at Uncle Ben's rice. A lot of people thought that it was owned by a black person or Aunt Jemima pancakes mix or syrup. Some people thought a black woman owned it."

As Larry spoke, Danny couldn't help but think back on the conversation he had with G when he asked if it wasn't a white person that actually owned the place.

Larry continued his rant, "now, we still have black people who are used today to do that very same thing. I want to hear of a black business that has mostly, if not all, black people that work for them. Then I can see how they are helping. Don't just give people a turkey for Thanksgiving day. Offer them a job that'll earn them dignity and respect. Black bosses, train and hire black people to sell your product. Then you will feel good knowing when you make money your people are also, like John Johnson did with Jet magazine or like Madam CJ walker did with her hair product."

"Wow, that's interesting Larry," said Danny. "I'm ashamed to say I thought that when I became rich, white people would see my money and respect my color."

Then G said, "Danny, how are you feeling right now?"

"I don't really know. I'm trying to process everybody's different points of view and being here in this house and seeing the Black American Village. I see everything in a new light."

"We are the same because we're black and yet we're not the same because of our experiences."

"I know I'm changing the subject a little but, here's what being rich was to me serving in Afghanistan, "Coming home alive with all of my limes still in tack. Trying to cope with survivor's guilt. I'm trying to fit into civilian life after the military. Now that I'm back home, not having a job is real. I'd love to be rich."

"Malik and Sam are friends who understand my struggle. They listen and talk to me. Malik gave me the opportunity to work in his shop. I give haircuts. I volunteer at the community center thanks to coach Matthew and I live with my sister and her family. I feel like Jesse. Do I deserve this kind of life?"

G looked at Danny with compassion, "of course, you deserve it all."

"Okay," G said, "I want everyone to get a pencil or pen and a piece of paper." The three men shuffled about the house in search of writing materials.

Larry looked over at Danny and said, "G is known for his stories." Danny smiled in remembrance of G's stories at the restaurant.

Chip handed a pen and paper to Danny. The rest settled with the same on the kitchen Island, expectantly waiting for G.

"Okay, everybody spread out. I want you to write this down. Everyone is starting out with $100,000. So write $100,000 on the top of your paper."

"Now, on the right side show how much money you'll have and on the left side of the paper show how much you've spent. Got that?"

"Yeah, Yeah, Yeah, Yeah," we answered.

"Okay! We are starting out with the same amount of money. Let's see how much you will all have left when this is over. Let's begin. We're going to the store to buy a car. You will search for your dream car. Now, your dream car costs $50,000. What will you do?"

"If you decide to buy your dream car, write down $50,000 in the left column. On the right side of the paper write down how much you have left. Now, we'll visit the expensive mall to buy $25,000 worth of clothes. If you decide to buy the clothes, on the left side of the paper, write down $25,000 then on the right side write down how much you have left."

"You are on your way to continue shopping and your favorite uncle calls you up on your cell phone and tells you he's giving you $10,000 for your birthday. He asks you to choose between cash or stock. Write down your preferences on the left and right columns."

The air was electric as they scrawled answers on the page. Danny felt a shift of energy that told him that everything would be fine from them onwards. Judging from the expressions on their faces, Danny knew they enjoyed the game, just as much as him.

G said, "moving on...you go to the store to buy the latest and largest TV, cell phone, computer and games. When you leave the store you've spent $10,000. You know the drill."

"Got that? Okay, while shopping you run into a friend of yours. He has just had great luck. He got his dream job in Hawaii and is making a lot of money but the catch is that he has to leave in ten days. He has to sell his family house that's fully rented out. He gets $1500 a month for each apartment. He gets an income of $54,000 a year. He has to sell it quickly and he's willing to sell it to you for $100,000 cash. Can you buy it?"

But, before you all can answer, including Danny.

"You get a phone call from your favorite uncle again. Hey, I'm going out of town for a month so I sold the stock. Each share cost $1.00 and I sold it for $10.00 a share. Now I have $100,000. I will wire the money into your account now. What do you tell your friend after the call?"

Larry quipped, "I'm buying the house."

G asked, "how much money do you have left Larry?"

Larry replied, "I bought everything. Since I optioned the stock, I've got a hundred grand. I got the money back."

"What about you Chip?"

"I brought the car and I wanted the cash and not the stock. So I only have $60,000 left."

"What about you Jesse?"

"Well you know me, I'm not taking any chances so I didn't buy anything, and didn't buy the stock. So, I've got $110,000. I can still afford the house."

"What about you Danny?"

"I brought the car and I took the $10,000 cash. I have $60,000 left. I should've bought the stock!"

"My answer to you and Jesse is, we are all worthy based on the decisions that we make. With me, you'll make money. It's up to you and your choices to become rich but I'll give you the leverage."

"Wow G," Chip said. "I never saw getting rich that way. I thought I had to just make a lot of money to get rich but if you make a lot of money and you spend it all you won't remain rich and if you make a lot of money and invest it in real estate or stocks you could remain rich because your money is growing."

Jessie said, "G that's why you invested in land and built here?"

"G has a continuing cash flow." Larry said.

"G, you have been a blessing to everyone in this community and it is blessing you right back."

"You keep winning G, because you have a good heart." Danny complimented. "Thank you, you've made me feel better about myself by allowing me to see that my decisions can lead me to success and I am worthy."

"I feel blessed that I listened to my sister Lola. She told me to create a *Go Fund Me* account. Now, look where I am because of that decision."

"Thanks to Savannah's gift, I played the scratch offs. Then relocated to North Carolina where I met Joy. Implementing her suggestions helped me enormously. Maya's summer fest helped me to visualize kid's programs for entrepreneurship which led to the Black Wall Street community."

"It's late. I'm going to take Danny back to the hotel. He's traveling back tomorrow and has to get up early."

"Nice meeting you, Danny."

"Thank you everyone, for making me feel welcome."

****

It was a clear day and Danny was downstairs in the hotel's restaurant waiting to have breakfast with G. When G arrived, he waved to draw his attention.

"Hi Danny. I'm sorry for keeping you waiting."

"No problem. I just got here five minutes ago."

"I hope you enjoyed your short stay?"

"I really did. Thank you so much for this big opportunity. I felt pretty hopeless when you first met me. This has been an amazing experience. Meeting your brother and friends was really nice. You brought me into your close circle. Not everyone gets that close to someone who is as rich as you."

G smiled, "I'm giving you two checks. This one is for $100,000 your payroll for the summer camp which you'll start by spring. Another $100,000 for you. I want you to focus on putting this program together, I'll take care of the bills. Now, it's time to build your business and team.

Close your *go fund me* page. you can't imagine the money you'll make. Danny, if you make the right choices you will be a millionaire. Have an attorney go over this contract, once you're certain, sign and get back to me."

"I feel like God has given me another chance. He used you to do this one. I would love to work with you. I will attach the business plans to the contract when I send it back to you G. I can't wait to see all of our plans come to fruition."

G held out his hand, and they shook on it. Relief at the success of their meeting, passed their features. They spent the next hour, eating and discussing. At the end, G dropped Danny off at the train station. He couldn't wait to get home to relay the good news to his family. Things had taken a turn for the better, miraculously.

Back Home

It was five in the evening when Danny got home.

"Hey, Lola I'm home."

"Danny! You're back! Welcome. I'm in the kitchen."

He dropped his bags by the door and rushed back to the kitchen, "I missed you guys," Danny told her.

"We missed you too. Come on over here and tell me everything. And don't leave nothing out. Please get the dishes and help me set the table." He walked over to the kitchen sink, ran the water and washed his hands.

"Lola, I don't know where to start."

"From the beginning," Lola prodded with excitement.

Danny started the story from the train station. When he mentioned Black America Village, she interrupted him.

"He built the place?"

"Yeah," Danny replied with all the surprise he'd felt back then, bubbling to the surface.

He rushed on to describe the community, without leaving out a single detail. She gasped when he mentioned the statues and murals. He talked about the camp, G's plans. Then to top it off, he told Lola that G owned the entire community. He was that rich. His sister's lips dropped open.

To deepen her shock, Danny added, "but wait, that's not all. He gave me 200k to start the business and my salary once contracts are signed I can deposit in the company's account!"

"What?! said Lola. I don't believe you."

"Here's the check." Danny unfolded the paper from his back pocket and showed it to her. "Oh wow, Danny this is serious. Now you have something for that business account we opened."

"Lola, G gave me part of the check for 100k so I could just focus on getting the curriculum developed by spring."

Lola's mouth dropped again. "I'm speechless Danny. This is happening so fast. I am so happy for you. What does he do for a living?"

"He developed commercial and residential properties and rented them out. Now, he's turning some of his land into a camp where kids can go for summer break. In between that, he'll rent the camp out for events. He wants me to hire veterans who'd teach the kids and share their stories."

"This is wonderful Danny," Lola laughed. We're here for you, whenever you need us. You know that don't you?"

"Yes, I know that and I feel that. I also realize that there'll always be challenges and it's how I can change the boiling water from me being a coffee bean into a beautiful aroma of coffee. That'll make the difference. Meeting G, his brother, friends and visiting Black America Village has made a big impact on me. I want to make a positive impact, be valuable to society. I want to bless you, the kids and Evan, like you guys have blessed me. I want mom and dad to be proud of me too."

"I'm sure they are."

Danny nodded, "so how has everyone been?"

Lola started telling all about the boys' escapades. Danny finished setting the table and arranged the food with the help of his sister.

"Is Danny home?!" Evan called from the living room.

"Yes, I'm here."

The boys sidled up to their uncle. They chatted about their weekend. Lola filled Evan on Danny's trip while they ate. Danny felt an inordinate amount of peace suffuse him. The events of the weekend and being with his family were surreal but he was ready to scoop it all in and let out the previous despair.

Veterans Kids Christmas Party

Danny was woken by his alarm the following morning. That and the clattering of Evan and the boys preparing for school. He stayed in his room until the house became quiet. While he planned the activities of his day, his phone rang.

"Hello," Danny whispered, blinking at Sam's name on the screen.

"Hey Danny, I'm glad you're back. What time do you get off from the shop?"

"Around noon. I don't have a lot of appointments today. Why? What's up?" Danny asked. He could hear Sam moving around.

"I'm off from the hotel. Gotta get Christmas presents for the Veteran's kids party. You wanna come along? Still going this year, right?"

"Sure. I'll go."

"I'll meet you back at your house and we will take my car," said Sam. "Then you can tell me everything that happened on your trip."

"You bet, see ya."

Danny hopped off the bed, woken by the prospects of the day. He'd spent the night plotting the camp plans. Though he slept late, he'd woken with more energy......

Getting to the shop, he forgot and glanced down into the hole on the floor, then jerked back in fear. Raucous laughter greeted his ears from the guys.

"Welcome back," Malik greeted, he was shaping up a customer's head.

"Thank you, brother."

"How was the trip?"

"It was insane. I have never experienced anything like it."

"Did you take any pictures?"

"Yeah, in my cell. You have to see this place Malik. It's an experience. It was filled with black culture and festive with positive vibes. With your skills I know you could even teach the kids at the camp there. You've been great to me; I can't wait to do the same for you. I tell you, G's doing big things."

"Let's talk about it Danny. I'll check out Black America Village, meet the guy before I decide to take up another shop."

"Bet you'll be surprised."

Few minutes later, Danny's first customer arrived.

"Good morning, good people," the guy greeted, gingerly avoiding the floor.

"Mornin'" The others chorused, their disappointment at the fact that he'd denied them a show was evident in their faces. Unfazed, the guy took his seat in Danny's chair.

"Are you listening to the Strawberry letter?" a new guy asked, nodding at the radio.

"Yeah, this guy told his girl that he wants out of the relationship. He's in love with someone else. Girl says she's pregnant. Now, he wants to know if he should tell the new girl about the baby or just say nothing."

"The second woman didn't know about the first woman when she started dating him," another customer added.

"Ouch!" Danny's client exclaimed. Everyone gave their opinion on the situation and agreed or disagreed with Steve Harvey's advice. By twelve, Danny stuffed his bag with his clippers and tools and said to Malik, "I'll see you tomorrow and don't forget we've got the vet's kids Christmas party tonight. "I got a gift for a boy," Malik said. "I'll be ready."

"Alright. I'm out,"

At the house, Sam's car was already parked out front. Quickly, Danny parked his vehicle, dropped his hair tool bag in the house and joined Sam.

"What's up my boy?!"

"Yo Sam, I can't stop thinking about this weekend. G's pretty loaded. Built this Black America Village. This place is like Black Wall Street, man! You hear me? How amazing is that?"

"Black Wall Street un-freaking-believable!" Sam pounded his steering wheel with a deep laugh. Danny, that's a dream come true, right there."

"You're right. You've got to meet him, man."

"What does the guy do for a living?"

"He was a schoolteacher. Then he won millions of dollars playing the scratch offs!"

"What!? Yo, I'm buying some today!"

"It wasn't just that he won but what he did with his winnings that intrigues me. I have never dreamed that big before. I talk about being rich all of the time. But being in G's world and seeing his efforts to build the community makes me view being rich differently."

"Sam, It's not all about partying, hanging out and spending money carelessly. It's about responsibility and accountability. I have never seen so many black people not worried about how they're going to pay their bills. Living in amazing houses, with the ability to buy stuff they want, anytime."

"How do you fit into all of this?" Sam asked, when Danny fell quiet.

"G's building a camp in Black America Village. But he needs someone to put life in it. Get it off the ground with a positive identity. He isn't sure which direction he wants the camp to go. So, he found me on my *Go Fund Me* page. Came to Claremont Hill and found me at your hotel restaurant! He liked how I envisioned his camp and asked me to join. He's paying and he has given me a budget for other veterans who would be interested in working there for the summer. During the summer I'll be filming the activities, to be sold online."

"I'll sell merch, like tee shirts and stuff to build out the brand. I'll hire a team that'll make appointments with different schools and inform them of the importance of hiring veterans to be mentors for their students. A lot of kids need someone to talk to and, get guidance. It could reduce the number of gangs and drugs. I think it'd be a win-win for us veterans and the students. Meanwhile I'll set up a center for kids to call for advice or just someone to talk to, while we wait to see if we can get into the schools."

"I'm so proud of you. Hope you're feeling good these days?"

"Yeah, thanks for asking. You and Lola are always looking out for me. I can only speak for myself but, the thought of suicide was not something that I planned. It was an irrational thought that I acted out because I was overwhelmed. I wondered if I'd have to struggle with the darkness for the rest of my life. That weighed on me."

"I just wanted to give up! Didn't want to fight anymore. It was like the class bully. Everyday over and over again he's picking on you. I thought I had no other option but to give up because I felt trapped not being able to start my life over again after being in the Army."

"My moment of clarity came when I talked to G. It helped me understand that there was always a way out, even when I was backed into a corner. Sam, most people I went to school with have a College degree now. I don't have one. I'm ashamed of that. I want to be respected. G's way of thinking helped me find my way out of the corner."

"I saw this tall Harriet Tubman statue. She faced fear, every step of the way with slaves and she went back and got more slaves risking her life. After talking with G, I saw that my thinking wasn't rational but at that moment it made sense. Wow, I was in danger Sam and I didn't even know it. How do you ask for help when you don't even realize you need help at that moment?"

"I never knew it was that bad, I was always here for you to talk to about it," Sam said, sounding like he'd failed Danny.

"I know and we talked many times, I felt like I had exhausted even you as an option. Sometimes it feels like when one struggle goes away here comes another one. Sam, I'm trying to find hope in the middle of my struggle. Now, I pray to Jesus Christ my Lord and Savior now. I started thinking about what slaves had to endure, way more than I have and, they made it through hard times with far less!"

"That's what I saw in Harriet Tubman's statue. I saw her courage in the midst of the storm. She walked right out of slavery and took black people with her over and over again. Like the white people who saw the Statue of Liberty, which represents freedom for them."

"Seeing that statue of Harriet Tubman with slaves behind her, In Black America Village, represented freedom for black people to me. Then seeing other statues of black people reminded me of the fights and killings they endured at that time so that we could be here and have a better life today. I felt a sense of pride being there."

"It was very insightful for G, to include black people's past in our present. We forget how strong we really are. Now, I kind a get that Ronald Smith's death wasn't my fault. He was a warrior and one of many black soldiers who died for his country. He looked fear in the face so others would know how too. There are a lot of civilians that will never know the feeling of facing that kind of fear."

"There is so much more to our black experience that we forget about. We are rich in culture, music, dance, singing, activism, scientists, scholars, entrepreneurs, and warriors and so much more. I can't wait for you to see it."

"Me too, Danny. Sounds wonderful."

"Now, where do we get the kid's presents? This year's gonna be splendid for them."

"We're going to a jewelry store."

"For Christmas gifts?"

"Yeah, I wanted to do something different."

"Okay."

We stopped by the store and we went our separate ways inside. My mind is empty. I was used to getting toys for my nephews. I'm not sure now. I see Sam checking out picture frames. I see these two lockets. This one stands out to me. It's gold with angel wings shaped like a heart. Oh wow the wings open up to show pictures inside of it. After seeing many other jewelries, I seem to be driven back to this angel locket with chips of sparkling crystals and diamonds that lace each gold wing and then stop in the middle of the wing and continue in gold. It opens up to put a picture also and has a gold plain back where I can put Loved.

"I found this diamond stainless steel bracelet for a boy. What about you?" Sam enquired.

"I'm not sure. I keep coming back to this necklace."

"I'll take this," Sam told the clerk. Unable to make a decision, I wandered a little more. I picked up the locket again and walked to Sam, "I think I'll take this. I want it to say *loved in* the back of the heart. I'll give it to a little girl." *I go* to pay at the counter.

"Lovely choice," said the clerk.

"Yes," I said, then I realized the clerk wasn't paying attention to me.

"I have a couple of lockets before yours that I have to inscribe, can you come back in an hour?"

"Oh, yes, I would like the word "loved" on the back."

"No problem," said the clerk. "You can pay now and come back in an hour and it will be ready." I paid and we walked out. "You know, Danny I like the gift but I feel like I should get something else."

"What do you think? Yeah, you're right. Let's go to the toy store on the other side of the mall."

"Sure, let's go."

"Let's see what they've got."

Inside the toy store, they split up again, they resembled kids strolling up and down the aisle. When they met up again, Danny asked, "what did you get?"

"I got him a skateboard with a helmet and kneepads. What about you?"

"I found this bubble gum machine that's like a bank and I have m&ms to put in it. I thought this would be cute for a girl's bedroom. Let's not forget to get wrapping paper."

"Oh, yeah. You're right."

"I'm really enjoying hanging out with you Danny."

The Christmas sounds, jingling bells, laughing kids rushing at dolls, all accumulated to a massive ball of happiness. The glow was contagious and soon, Sam and Danny found themselves grinning sheepishly at each other.

"I'm kind of excited to bring happiness to some kid."

"It does feel good," Sam agreed.

After they'd picked out a ton of toys and stored them in Sam's car, they returned to the jewelry shop. It was chock full with buyers. When it got to their turn, the clerk was still busy with several orders.

Danny called his attention by tapping the counter, "hi, I'm here to pick up a gold wings heart locket with *"loved"* engraved on the back. The clerk grabbed the first bag in front of him and handed it to me.

Since the store was crowded, I didn't want to make trouble and assumed the bag would contain my order. I accepted the receipt and walked out with Sam.

"I gotta get the boys from the community center. Can you drop me off at home, so I can get my car?"

"Yeah," Sam said, "I've got a few things to do before the party tonight."

"A'ight. But you gotta pick me up later. We should go together."

"No worries. Can't wait to see the kids' faces."

They boarded the car and sang along to Kirk Franklin's

Imagine me all the way.

An Angel Sent by God

Danny was getting dressed in his room. Liam and Lucas watched him from the bed. They were under strict orders not to bounce on the mattress. To distract them, he selected two turtle neck sweaters and held them against his chest, "come on boys, which one should I wear?"

"The black one!" Lucas shouted.

Danny said with a grin, "thank you."

"That one sucks, Uncle Danny. The white one with your navy v neck sweater and dark blue jeans and your navy peacoat is best, especially with that nice hair cut and smile you have."

"Hmmm, sorry Lucas. I'm going with Liam on this one tonight."

"Yeah, I agree." Liam quipped.

Lola peeked in through the door, "here, Danny your gifts are wrapped."

"Thank you, I don't know what I'd do without you guys."

"I see the boys are helping you get dressed as always."

"Yes, they even picked out the cologne that I'm gonna to wear." Lola giggled.

"Okay, boys," she said, "let's leave Uncle Danny alone so he can finish preparing. Sam will be here before you know it. Have a good time tonight."

"Thank you Lola."

"Good night guys. I'll tell you all about it tomorrow."

"Okay," the boys said. As they left, they darted crestfallen eyes at Danny. Their little shoulders slouched in disappointment.

Thirty minutes later, Danny was ready and his cell rang, almost on cue.

"What's up man? I'm outside, you ready?"

"A'ight cool, I'm on my way out."

Danny gathered the wrapped gifts and headed out after bidding his family another goodnight.

"Woah! You look nice, dude." said Sam

"Thanks," Danny said, as he shut the door. "My boys got me dressed."

"Again, Danny? I'm gonna need them to help me get dressed too." They shared a laugh.

Sam pulled into the road and they were on their way. "Malik said he'll meet us there. I think he's bringing his girl."

"I'm nervous, Sam and I don't know why. This is my first veteran's Christmas party. Do you think I should have gotten different gifts?"

"Stop worrying. The gifts you got are beautiful. You'll be fine."

At the venue, Sam waved at a friend after he'd parked the car. He told Danny to get his gifts while he greets the friend he'd not seen in a long time and he'll meet him inside.

"Okay." Danny agreed, he gathered his wrapped boxes and walked up the stairs. There was a bald headed nice looking guy, at the double doors. He stopped Danny inside of the entrance of the venue.

Danny smiled at him over the gifts, "Hello, I'm here for the veteran's kids Christmas party."

"Alright," the security guard leaned down and took out a bouquet of yellow roses from the concierge desk which he placed on top of one of Danny's boxes. "For the parents. Everyone leaves with something tonight."

"Wow, that's thoughtful. I wouldn't have thought of that."

The man smiled his thank you and ushered Danny into a room full of kids and grateful parents. Christmas music blasted from the speakers. The room was decorated in silver and gold colors. There were tables set up all around the room. Occasional piercing squeals rent the hall as kids tore open their presents.

"See that little girl, sitting next to her mom?"

"Yeah."

"She didn't get a gift yet. She looks a little sad," said the security guard. "I'm sure you would put a smile on her face and make her mother happy with these yellow roses."

Danny bobbed his head and lowered the gifts to the floor. Children, held back by their parents, watched him with nervous energy. He shook the guard's hand, wondering where he'd seen the man before.

"No problem, I'm glad I could help. Just remember, "You, have been blessed, to be a blessing."

When the guard left, Danny mustered courage to approach the little girl and her mother. "Hello, my name is Danny. I saw you sitting here and I wanted to bring your daughter some Christmas gifts."

The kid looked to her mother for approval, the woman gave it with a gentle smile. Danny brought the gifts and handed them to the grinning kid.

"We came at the last minute so we really didn't expect any presents," the mother was saying as her daughter tore the wrapping. "I just thought it'd be good to be around other people who have lost a loved one that was in the military."

"I'm glad you came out," Danny assured her, "and these are for you," Danny passed the yellow roses to her. He was grateful once more to the guard for the yellow roses because of the beatific smile that graced the woman's face.

"Thank you. They're my favorite."

Danny spotted a button on the floor, he picked it up, "is this yours?

She stared at the medium-sized brown button and back at Danny, "no, but I'll take it." Her lips held the ghost of a smile as she turned the button in her palm. "It's funny, my husband always called me button. He'd say I had a button nose. H-he was killed in active service. These yellow roses are beautiful. My husband sometimes surprised me with them."

Danny didn't know whether to chuckle or settle for sad, "What a crazy coincidence. I'm sorry about your husband. Uh, can I sit with you?"

"Yes, please," the woman replied. The little girl suddenly gave a high-pitched squeal of her own, startling both of them. The mother took the locket and gazed at Danny with her eyes misting. Immediately, Danny began to worry that he'd gotten the wrong gift. The girl loved it but it seemed to make her mother sad.

She whispered, "Who are you?"

"A veteran, no kids though. My name's Danny. It's my first one, I felt led to come but now, I think I should've gotten something else. I'm sorry. I can get her another gift."

"No, you don't understand. I was led to come tonight also. Thank you for this blessing you have given us. You sent her a message that I know her father would've wanted her to know."

"He would?" Danny repeated, looking puzzled.

The mother stared at the locket and read the inscription, *"I'll be with you always love dad."* written on the back."

Danny's heart thumped with surprise, "can I see that?"

Danny turned the jewelry in his hand. The clerk had given him the wrong order, yet it turned out to be perfect. It was certainly beyond him. He could feel God's work in the entire process.

"Here you go, kid. Your dad really loves you," Danny said, stumbling over the words. The mother tapped his arm affectionately.

"Thank you," she said. She hooked the necklace around her daughter's neck.

The young girl started to tear up the second wrapping. "Mommy!" she squealed, "look it's me and daddy's favorite candy in a gumball machine."

The little girl bounced up and threw her tiny frame at Danny. Her mother was on the verge of tearing up again.

"My pleasure," Danny said, patting her dark head. The kid gave him the cutest smile. The smile melted something within him. His responding smile was almost involuntary, effortless. Danny glanced at the mother, who was once again, playing with the button.

"I feel like my husband is here and he sent you to let us know he loves us and he is okay. I'm so glad that we came."

"I'm glad too."

Danny broke their locked eyes and focused on the kid. He tapped her little button nose, "what was your daddy's name?" he asked her.

"Sergeant Ronald Smith!" she answered with glee, quite pleased with herself. "It's my baby brother's name too."

Danny's heart slammed against his chest, "wh-what'd you s-say?" he stuttered.

"Ron Smith," the mother confirmed.

Danny's eyes went wide, he swallowed hard and asked with trepidation, "was he in 82nd Airborne division? Did he serve in Afghanistan?"

"That's where he uh...you know," she said, darting a worried glance at her kid.

What were the odds?

Danny sat still, frozen with another astounding coincidence that'd happened to him. How could this woman be Ron's family? The button, the yellow roses, the locket, the m&ms, and now? The Ron that got shot right next to me. Then it occurred to me that I had to tell her about Ron and that chilled me even more. The peeks of that guilt began to slip out. I couldn't keep quiet though, despite the wedge lodged in my throat, I had to tell them.

"I knew him. Uh...I was w-with him when it happened," he blurted.

"Oh my God!" The woman cried in astonishment. "I prayed I'd talk to someone who was with him. I prayed for a sign, lord, I wanted to know that he is okay now and I got you." Tears slid down her cheeks, unabashed.

"Mommy are you okay?" her child asked, eyes melting with worry. She hugged the kid.

Danny's hands trembled with slams of guilt, "I'm so sorry. I couldn't save him. If he had not followed me, he'd be alive. I'm so sorry." Danny bowed his head in shame, afraid to see the judgment in her eyes.

She clasped his shaking hands, Danny made to withdraw but she kept steady until he looked at her. Her eyes, though reddened with tears, were filled with empathy. Some of the distress eased from Danny's chest.

She said, "how could you have saved him? Are you God and could see the future? You couldn't save yourself, you were both in danger."

Danny hands reduced their shivering within her warm grasp, *you couldn't save yourself.* She was right. Literally. Another soldier had actually pulled me from danger.

She continued, "both of you were shot at. You had no idea that it'd happen at that moment, or it could've been prevented. My husband is safe now with God, I feel God sent you here so we could know that. It's your time to let God's light shine through you by how you serve others. You are blessed to be a blessing. My husband would've wanted you to know that."

I tried to stop my prickling eyes from filling with water but it was impossible in the face of her kindness. An impossible weight lifted from my chest as I met her unwavering gaze. I needed to meet her. My nerves disappeared as a wobbling smile quirked up her lips. She released my hands and patted her kid's head. A surge of relief roared through me as globs of tears slicked past my defenses.

"Thank you," he whispered, "you don't know what you've done for me." he said putting a herculean effort into pulling himself together.

"Look at God," she smiled through the tears. "He's good all the time."

"You have a boy too?"

"Yes, I'd gotten pregnant the last time I saw Ron on his two-week break. I didn't find out that I was pregnant until after the funeral."

"It must've been very hard to raise both of them."

"It is. It is also beautiful. But honestly, I had help from friends and my mother. Even tonight, mom's watching Ronny while we get some girl's time."

"Ronald told me that he wanted a son one day. His dream came true."

"He told you that?"

"Yes, he did."

"He told everyone who cared to listen or not about his wife and daughter. He loved you very much. I'm so grateful that I got a chance to see you and your daughter.

Please I'd like to have your phone number, I'll be working at a summer camp. I'll give you all of the information when it's closer to the time. I would love for your daughter to visit."

"I'd love that too, but how much does the camp cost?"

"Don't worry about it. I got you."

"Are you sure? I think she would love that. Right baby?" The kid gave a vigorous nod. Danny beamed at her.

"Then she'll be there. Here's my cell phone number."

"Thanks. I'll be in touch."

"I'm going to place a picture of my baby and her dad in the locket. Thank you again, Danny." We shared a smile. The party was certainly a blessing. It was his first time and it'd been beyond his expectation.

Danny spotted Sam approaching them. "There you are," he said when he arrived. "been looking all over the place for you."

"Hey Sam. I've been with this lovely family. This is ... oh I never got your name..."

"Nicole Smith and this is my daughter, Tracy."

"Hello, nice to meet you," Sam said, shaking her hand.

"You guys, go on and have a good time. Please, Danny, stay in touch. I would really like my daughter to go to the camp."

"I will, I have your number, I promise." Danny rose from the table and scraped back his chair, "Good night Tracy, Nicole."

Sam stared at Danny, "Hey, are you okay?"

"Sure," Danny assured him with a firm nod. He'd never felt better. His steps, as they approached the door, were light as air.

"I just want to thank the security guard."

"What security guard?"

"The one manning the door, when you came in. Did he leave early?"

Sam shot Danny a puzzled glance. Danny frowned at him, "he was passing out roses, for goodness sake. Didn't you get roses?"

Sam spoke slowly, "There was no security guard at the entrance. No roses either."

Danny shook his head and jogged the rest of the way to the door. Sam, are you sure you didn't see a bald headed nice looking black guy at the door? No Danny, I didn't see him. He scanned the place, including the parking lot. The security guard is gone.

"Well, he was here. Maybe he went to the bathroom. I'll just wait here for a few minutes."

He saw a waiter passing with a tray of drinks, "excuse me, where's the security guard?"

The waiter passed a bewildered glance between Sam and Danny, "there is no guard."

"Are you sure?"

"Yes, I'm sure, there was no security guard posted at the door. What was he doing? Are the kids safe?"

"Yes...yes," Danny said distractedly. The waiter shook his head and continued on his way.

The Answer

Danny stared at Sam, "You're certain. You didn't see a bald headed nice looking Black guy? He looked like I'd seen him before but I couldn't place him."

No Danny. "Do you want to go Danny, and get something to eat?" Sam asked concernedly.

"I've given my gifts to a young boy. Let's get something to eat at the Waffle House."

"Yeah, I don't know what's going on." was my vague response. My confusion continued all the way to the car. I'm trying to wrap my brain around what is happening. I'm glad that you are driving Sam, because my head is flooded trying to figure this out. At the Waffle house, Sam asked him why he'd been so quiet on the ride here.

"I'm sorry Sam. I *know* there was a security guard there because he gave me yellow roses *and* he pointed me to that table you found me."

After they took their seats and placed an order. Danny leaned forward and told Sam, "you won't believe this. That lady? Nicole..."

"Yeah?" Sam said warily.

"Well, her husband was the guy who died by my side in Afghanistan."

"No way!"

"Yes! " and the security guard pointed her out to me and gave me the yellow roses for her. I gave Tracy, the daughter, the Christmas presents."

"Danny...woah, that's weird. And it was the absent security guard that gave you the roses?" you look just as bewildered as me.

"Sam, I got the wrong locket. It said *I will be with you always, love dad* on the back. I told the guy to write "*loved*," remember?"

"Yo Danny, this is starting to sound a little eerie don't you think?"

"Then there was the brown button that I found on the floor near her table and I gave it to her. Then she tells me that her husband used to call her button. Then the consoling words of insight she said to me. I was captivated by hearing her point of view of how she saw what happened in Afghanistan. Sam, I can't lie bro. I felt like a ton of weight was lifted off me after we spoke."

"Danny, this has to be a blessing from God man! He sent one of his Angels down here to hook you up." "Sam! That's it!." "I remember where I saw the security guard before."

"Where, Danny?" sitting on the edge of my seat too.

"This might sound crazy but he resembled one of the angel statues stationed outside of G's gated community Black America Village."

Sam jumped out of his seat and then sat just as fast. "No way! This is not happening! Yo, I need a drink Danny. We should've gone to a sports bar instead."

Perplexed, I can't utter a word. I'm trying to understand why all of this is happening to me. Nearly missed hitting a woman, her child and could have killed myself. The coincidental meeting with G, the camp, Ron's family, m&ms and the security guard. Even the roses and the button were enigmas. Lola prays for me all of the time, every chance she gets. Suddenly Danny's back straightened as a memory slammed into him.

"I remember she fell to the floor in the kitchen and Lola cried out to God, and asked God for a miracle. The boys came into the kitchen to check on her because they heard cry out. I'd never seen her so broken as she was in the kitchen that night."

"Sam, I am sitting here astonished. Lola's is an intercessor. Really Danny?"

I can't stop beaming. I am humbled and grateful. There is a peace beyond my understanding that is settling in over me. "Yeah. Oh my God, yes Sam. I think...No, I *know* God answered Lola's prayer for me and I am humbled, thankful and grateful."

The End.

www.ingramcontent.com/pod-product-compliance
Lightning Source LLC
Chambersburg PA
CBHW050925030726
47503CB00007BB/2467